SNOWED IN WITH THE GARGOYLES
A MONSTROUS HOLIDAY TALE

CLEARWATER MONSTERS

ZOE ASHWOOD

Copyright © 2024 by Zoe Ashwood

All rights reserved.

No part of this book may be reproduced in any form or by any electronic or mechanical means, including information storage and retrieval systems, without written permission from the author, except for the use of brief quotations in a book review.

Cover by Bia Shuja.

Edited by Emmy Ellis of Studioenp.

Proofread by Lori Parks.

Created with Vellum.

A LETTER TO MY READERS

Hi!

Thank you so much for picking up another Monstrous Holiday Tale! *Snowed in with the Gargoyles* is a MMF story, meaning our heroine gets two heroes and doesn't have to choose between them.

This is a cozy, spicy romance with inhuman heroes. If you need to check the content warnings for this series, you can find them on my website.

You don't have to read *Stranded with the Kraken* to enjoy *Gargoyles* - all the books in this series are complete stand-alones, though characters from other books might be mentioned.

Enjoy your book!

xo, Zoe

CHAPTER 1

MORGAN

I pull the hood of my parka close and wonder if I should just give up. It's freezing, the snowstorm is relentless, and unless I start moving, my fingers and toes might fall off. I shouldn't have come here tonight, on Christmas Eve of all times, but I *think* I've finally found what I've been searching for.

My snow boots crunch in the thick layer of snow, plunging straight through a drift. I stumble and just manage to catch myself on a frosty tree trunk. The movement dislodges a load of fresh, powdery snow from the branches, and it falls right on top of me, dusting my knit hat and shoulders in white.

This is dangerous.

The voice of reason in my head sounds shriller by the minute, and I'll have to give in soon, I know it. When I traced the strange sightings of a giant winged creature to the old watchtower at Blarney Hill above the sleepy little town of

Clearwater, Maine, I never thought I'd be stalking the place in such shitty weather. My friend, Arielle, was the one who told me the local legend about the watchtower being haunted, and I knew I had to check it out. I'm *this* close to making my big discovery, and I don't want the creature to move on if this isn't its permanent residence.

Besides, I'm sure the chance of getting some nice shots is higher tonight than in good weather—no one in their right mind would venture out in this cold. So if the creature really *is* living in this decrepit old building, they're home now. I just have to get close enough to the tower to see through all this snow, preferably before it gets completely dark. Lighting my flashlight would be a dead giveaway, and I'd rather not alert them to my presence before I'm ready.

My phone chimes. I take it from my pocket and tug my glove off with my teeth. It's another text from Arielle, telling me that she's still with her hookup from the app for monster dating. I'm glad she's checking in to tell me she's safe, but my battery is dying—probably the cold leaching its life faster than usual—so I just type back a thumbs-up and tuck my phone away.

I'm nowhere near ready to start dating again. What I need to do is focus on my career, not waste time on men, whether it's humans or monsters.

I really should turn back.

The visibility is getting worse by the minute, and when I look back at my tracks, a jolt of worry goes through me at the thought that they might get covered in a fresh layer of snow. The farther I get from the road, the bigger the chance that I'll get lost. It would be the height of stupidity to die of exposure just two miles from the town because I was too stubborn to give up on a potentially huge discovery.

The truth is, I'd imagined myself in a different place by

now. I'd finished my degree in conservation biology and scored a place on a national project for bat conservation along with my handsome fiancé—and I thought life couldn't get any better. We had a five-year plan to get married and have two kids before I turned thirty because we both wanted to be young parents.

Turns out, Andy's five-year plan also included banging some woman he met at the gym, which he failed to inform me about. When I confronted him, it wasn't just my love life that fell apart—he was the senior scientist on the project, so they kept him on while I was left scrambling to find a new job at a time when all the funding for the year had already been distributed and no one was taking on new personnel.

I'd spent a miserable two weeks on my parents' couch in Richmond, sending my résumé to anyone even remotely connected with my field, and eating my weight in Mom's pierogi. Finally, I found a job at an ecological agricultural company in Clearwater, one where I could work in my field, even if it wasn't as exciting as bat conservation.

It's been…a challenge. My mental health hasn't been that great, and I've been trying to dig myself out of my rut, both by hanging out with Arielle and by researching this supposedly supernatural creature haunting the old tower.

That doesn't mean I should pick death by snow voluntarily. If I don't make it out of here soon, I won't get a chance to get better. I glare at the dark shape of the tower through the trees. I've been staring at it from as close as I dared, waiting for movement, for any indication that it was occupied, but nothing happened. Now it's too late, so I stomp my foot angrily, then turn one hundred and eighty degrees and start making my way back.

I was right about my footsteps being obscured. If I'd waited any longer, they would have been gone completely, and in the quickly falling twilight, I never would have found my car. As it is, I have to squint in the dimming light that's hell on my eyes—not helped by the fact that my glasses are dotted with melted snowflakes and fogged up from my choppy breaths.

In my hurry to return to safety, I forget about the snowdrift I'd encountered before. I plow straight on, and the ground disappears from underneath me. My boot sinks through, I face-plant into a thick snowy pillow, and bright, stabbing pain shoots through my leg.

My mouth is full of snow. I get my hands underneath me and try to push up, but my leg hurts too badly. I whimper and slowly roll to the side. I swipe my gloved hands over my face, then take off my glasses and shake off most of the snow. It doesn't help much, but it's something I *can* do. Then I grit my teeth and gingerly pull my leg out of the snowdrift.

There are branches underneath the snow—I feel them brushing up against my snow pants. I don't want to tug too fast—if I cut myself on top of whatever injury I've already sustained, it'll be that much worse for me. So I shift back slowly, careful not to sink back through the drift. I inch my leg out and move my ass toward the nearest tree, assuming the ground will be more firm there, with less snow layered under the branches.

It hurts. A lot. The pain, which radiated so suddenly through my leg, is now centered in my ankle, a throbbing sting that tells me it's at least badly sprained if not broken. I'm no doctor, but even I know this is bad. I was already pushing my luck with staying out here for so long, but now? I'll freeze to death before anyone finds me.

My foot finally slips free of the hole, and I whimper as I bump my boot on a hidden branch. Yep, the ankle is fucked all right. Gritting my teeth, I scoot farther back so I can rest against the tree trunk, then pull my gloves off and reach for my phone.

I have only twenty percent of the battery left, but the little yellow bar has me exhaling with relief—it's enough to call 911 and let the emergency team know where I am.

But when I hold my phone up to my ear, all I get is a busy signal. I try again, and again, but the call won't go through.

I face the gray sky, watching the millions of large snowflakes drifting down. The storm must have knocked down the towers or else everyone is calling the emergency services, because this kind of weather makes for more accidents.

The realization of just how screwed I am settles in slowly. I put my phone away and tug on my gloves. Then I zip up my parka to my chin and put on the hood that fell off while I was rolling around on the ground. I know I need to keep my body warmth—and get to shelter, fast.

Now it's time to make the hard decisions, but the pulsing pain in my ankle makes that so much harder. It fuels my body with adrenaline, along with a shot of panic, because I know I might actually die if I make the wrong choice. Not the best mindset to be making life-altering decisions, but it's all I've got, so I take several deep breaths through my nose and try to calm myself.

My car is about three quarters of a mile away. I parked on one of the service roads that cut through the forest, hiked along it for maybe half a mile, then cut through the forest toward the tower. I didn't want to alert the tower's occupants to my presence, so I couldn't risk bringing my car too close.

The walk was pleasant enough while it was still light out and I had the use of both of my legs, but in the falling twilight and with a bum ankle, it would take at least twice as long. Not to mention the fact that my footsteps from earlier are disappearing fast, and even though I have a map and compass in my backpack, that won't do me much good. It's so easy to get turned around in the dark.

That reminds me…

I take my backpack off and root through it for my flashlight. I changed the batteries yesterday, when I was preparing for this trip and putting together an emergency kit, but I don't switch it on yet. As long as I have at least some visibility, I should save it.

Instead, I shoot off a message to Arielle, telling her I'm stuck—but as expected, the app lets me know within seconds that it hasn't been sent.

An overwhelming sense of solitude almost crushes me. I'm all alone here, and no one knows exactly where I am. I told Arielle I was researching this tower, and I let my neighbor, Mrs. Rowell, know I was going hiking, but she won't even know I'm missing until she wakes up in the morning and realizes I haven't checked in with her. Now that I've watched the ruin for an hour, I'm thinking all the sightings of supernatural creatures were just the result of people's overactive imagination and scary stories told to misbehaving kids.

But I could still shelter inside.

It's old and decrepit looking, for sure, but it's a stone building that's stood here for centuries, so I suppose it has weathered more than one such storm in its lifetime. If I could get inside, I'd be out of the snow, and if I'm lucky, I might find enough dry kindling to make a fire.

I squint through the snow at the looming dark shape. It's not far—but with my leg, the distance still won't be an easy one to cross.

I stuff my flashlight in my backpack. The faster I get moving, the better. I don't want to get too chilled, or the cold will start affecting my decision-making.

Gritting my teeth, I put all my weight on my good leg and

hold on to the tree trunk to get upright. It hurts like hell, and I'm not even putting any weight on my busted ankle. It's as if gravity is enough to make it hurt worse, throbbing in time with my quickened heartbeat.

"Crap."

I hop on one foot, still holding on to the tree. The pain spikes, almost unbearable. I should wrap the ankle or something, but the thought of sitting again and pulling off my boot in this cold fills me with dread. Suddenly, I'm sure that I only have one chance at getting to safety, so I can't squander it.

The next tree is only a couple of feet away. I can do this.

I hobble forward until I'm only touching the first tree trunk with my fingertips, then let go and pitch myself toward the next one. I barely catch myself, my gloved hands scrabbling on the icy tree bark, but I manage to keep upright.

The pain is a constant ache now, and I know I might not have the will to get up again if I fall. So I repeat the process, zigzagging this way and that, wobbling from tree to tree.

After several such passes, I'm sweating under my winter clothes, my breaths sawing painfully in and out of my lungs. Every inhale burns my throat. But I'm making progress, and I mustn't let the pain get me down.

Then I glance back to see how far I've come, and the hope dies in my chest. The first tree, the one by the snowdrift, is barely thirty feet away. I've spent all this energy, endured all this pain, and only traveled this far?

I search for the abandoned tower again. It's not far, but in these conditions, it might as well be miles away. Have I made a mistake by choosing to go in this direction?

I waver on my feet, so close to giving in to the urge that's telling me to sink to the ground, to roll up and rest, if only for a minute. A rational part of my brain is screaming at me, telling me why that would be a terrible idea, but I just hurt so much.

A shape moves somewhere above me. It's only a flicker I catch in the corner of my eye, but it sends a jolt of awareness through me. I turn instinctively, and the pain blooms again, brighter than before. My leg goes out from under me, and I tumble to the ground, my gloved hands sinking into the snow.

"Ah!"

I yelp, then press my lips together, trying to keep quiet. It might have just been a bird, but I did come into these woods to research the haunting of the Blarney Hill tower, so I need to be careful just in case.

Tears leak from my stinging eyes as I try to scramble upward again. I could just yell for help—not that I think anyone else is dumb enough to be out here in this weather. But it's either that or freeze to death, and I'm not about to go down without a fight. Mrs. Rowell might try to call the rescue for me, but if the phones are down for the entire town, she won't be able to get anyone on the line. And besides, I don't think the emergency services would be able to spare as many people as it would take to do a proper search of the forest.

By the time they made it here, I'd be frozen solid for sure. Or mauled by some hungry forest animal.

The thought of being found by search dogs is what spurs me onward. I crawl a couple of feet, but this is even worse than hopping because my ankle drags along the ground, bumping painfully. I make it to another tree and grip its cold trunk to heave myself to my feet again when a dull *whump* interrupts the silence.

My heart stops for a moment, then skitters in a faster beat, all my senses on high alert. On instinct, I press myself closer to the tree, not that the young maple would be able to hide me.

Then I look up, just in time to see a massive shape hurtle from the sky, straight between the tree trunks. A heavy weight slams onto the ground twenty feet from me.

The creature crouches low, then unfurls to its full height, its wings fanning out.

"Hello," it says. "Do you need help?"

CHAPTER 2

MORGAN

It's a demon.

A demon has come for me straight from Hell.

"N-no," I choke out. "I-I don't want—I was good. You can't take me."

I'm not dead yet—and I'm definitely not ready to be dragged down to the fiery pits. Maybe I didn't go to church every Sunday, and maybe I dodged Mrs. Rowell one time too many when she tried to get me to look at the photos of her many, many cats, but surely that doesn't mean I'm facing eternal torture?

Then I remember the lustful thoughts I had about my Marine Biology professor in college, even though he was a married man, and realize that yep, this is it. Not to mention the collection of filthy, explicit romances taking up way too much space on my e-reader.

The demon cocks its horned head to the side, shadows hiding its face. "What?"

I clear my throat. "If you're here to take me to Hell, I

would like to ask you to reconsider. As you can see, I'm not dead yet, and, uh, I have someplace else to be."

A choked laugh comes from the creature. Then it steps closer, and in the last light of the day, I make out a gray-skinned, rough-hewn face, a broad, muscled chest—naked, even in these freezing conditions—and wide, leathery wings.

Bat wings.

My heart skips a beat, and a tiny sprout of hope springs to life in my chest as my panic recedes slightly. The creature is not dragging me into a brimstone-filled fiery pit, which is definitely helping my nerves.

"I'm not a demon, human," he says, for *it* is a *he*, at least I think so, with a male physique and a deep, rumbling voice.

"You're not?" I squeak.

He puts his hands on his hips and stares down at me. "No. I am a gargoyle."

His English is lightly accented, maybe German or one of the other European languages I can't speak. The low timbre of his voice is calming, though, as if meeting an injured woman in the forest is completely normal for him.

And maybe it is. Maybe gargoyles prey on unsuspecting hikers, then do unspeakable things to them in that tower.

Because I'm sure now that *this* is the source of all the local legends.

"Don't be afraid," he says. "I won't hurt you."

"That's what they all say," I grumble, but I study him all the same, my professional curiosity flaring to life.

I *did* work on a bat conservation project, and this guy has massive bat wings. They're growing out of his back, though, and he has a pair of arms, unlike bats. They don't have front legs, or rather, their arms have evolved into wings, with membranes connecting their bones.

Of course, my mind is spouting bat facts as a coping mechanism. I should be screaming for help, and instead, I'm admiring the stunning lines of this creature's humerus, which must be longer than my femur, judging by his wingspan.

I try to pull myself up, but my leg is killing me. Staying in one place for so long has been a mistake. I'm getting chilled, especially because I sweated through my base layers earlier.

"Who says what?" the gargoyle asks, now visibly confused.

I groan and drop back to my hands and knees. "Serial killers. I'm easy prey. Please don't take advantage of me."

The gargoyle crouches next to me, though he's still much larger, his head above my eye level.

"I promise not to hurt you," he repeats. "But if you remain here, you might die. You humans are so fragile. I saw you limping. You won't make it out of the forest on your own."

My chest tightens at the realization that he's right. I need his help, even though I don't know if I can trust him.

Slowly, the gargoyle extends his hand, palm up, a clear offer of assistance. I hate that I put myself in this situation—that I have to accept it or die, that putting myself in a potentially even more dangerous situation is my only choice.

I grimace, then hold my finger up. "Just a moment."

I tug off my glove and try my phone again. It's a double test—first to see if the network is up, and second to make sure he won't try to knock my phone away or steal it from me to prevent me from calling for help. He doesn't, but the call doesn't go through either, so I guess I'm stuck here for the moment.

Gingerly, I put my hand in his much larger one. His fingers close around mine, warm and leathery. A jolt of awareness goes through me at the contact—he's so much larger than me, and stronger, he could crush me easily.

But he holds my hand like it's precious, even though his dark, thick eyebrows draw together in a frown.

"You're freezing," he barks.

I look down at myself, as if to say, duh. I've been crawling through snow, of course I'm freezing.

But he's already moving, standing to his full height. "I will take you to our roost. Get you warm first. Then I will fly you to your human house."

Oh.

Maybe he won't try to kill me after all?

"Okay." I grasp his hand a little tighter and lift myself onto my knees. "That-that sounds good."

I try to stand again, but my ankle won't have it. I sway to the side, but the gargoyle is there, catching me by my shoulders. He's quick, much quicker than I would have guessed given his size. Now that I'm mostly upright, he towers over me, my eyes level with his very naked chest. His only item of clothing is a pair of leather pants that do little to hide his amazing shape.

Realizing I'm staring at his crotch, I jerk my head up and smash the top of my head into his chin—because he has leaned closer and is clearly sniffing me.

"Whoa, big guy," I yelp, reeling back. "No funny business."

"I am sorry," he growls, though he doesn't drop me. "Did I hurt you?"

I rub my head through my knit hat and hood. "I'm fine."

He hesitates for a moment, then asks, "Can I pick you up? It will hurt less and get us there much faster."

I want to protest. There's no way this is safe. But staying out here isn't an option either, and I don't want to die. Even though going along with this strange man's—gargoyle's—plan might be dangerous, it's safer than remaining out here alone.

"Yeah," I say finally. "Thanks. But please watch out for my leg. I sprained my left ankle. Might be broken, I don't know yet."

The gargoyle hums. "We will get you to a hospital soon."

I cringe at the thought of medical bills that might be added to my mountain of student loans. Being made redundant didn't do much good for my credit score. "Maybe it's just a bad sprain. I hope."

He narrows his eyes in suspicion, staring at me for a moment. Then he bends at the waist and picks me up in a quick swoop, and suddenly, I'm in his arms, cradled against his naked chest.

My mind registers the warmth of his skin, but my body reacts first, softening and relaxing. His scent reminds me of wood fires and coziness, and some primitive part of my brain must equate that with safety. I breathe in through my nose, then realize I'm behaving just as oddly as he was a minute ago.

Mortified, I lift my gaze to find him watching me with a small smirk tugging up the corner of his mouth. It's not a full smile, more an acknowledgment that he indeed saw me sniffing him.

Damn it.

"Er, thank you," I say. "I hope I'm not too heavy."

He shakes his head, his horns now barely visible in the darkness. "You're not." His grip on me tightens, and he adds, "Hold on, human."

Then he spreads his huge wings and launches us into the air.

"Eep!"

I let out a yelp and clutch his naked shoulders, legs flailing out. It's a stupid thing to do, both because I could fall and because my ankle jolts with pain once more. I whimper and scrunch my eyes closed, turning my face into the gargoyle's chest.

"I'm sorry." His voice rumbles against my ear. "I should have warned you."

I don't dare open my eyes, not that I would see much. I'm being pelted with snowflakes, my half-frozen cheeks stinging with the sensation. "I thought we'd walk."

Another thump of his strong wings. "The only entrance to the tower is from the top. There is no door on the ground level."

This new tidbit of information has me looking up at him. "So there's no exit?"

"No," he confirms. "But you only need to say the word, and Emmerich or I will fly you out immediately. You will not be caught in there."

"Who's Emmerich?" I demand.

But the gargoyle remains completely calm as he answers, "My roost mate. You will meet him soon. He will not hurt you either."

My mind is at war with my body. I'm clearly entering a strange situation with two supernatural creatures, so I should be shouting for help and ordering him to take me to town. At the same time, I've never been more relaxed. Maybe this is the gargoyles' way of luring in their prey. Do they secrete a chemical that calms their unsuspecting victims? There are countless cases from the animal kingdom to support my theory.

My analytical brain buzzes with the questions, already planning on interrogating them. Yet no matter how hard I try to rouse myself and fight this cozy sensation, I can't bring myself to do it. In truth, this gargoyle hasn't done anything untoward yet. And even if I tried to escape, I'd have nowhere to go. Not to mention he's much stronger than me—and currently flying me forty feet above the ground.

In the darkness, the old tower materializes, the roof covered in snow. The gargoyle lands on a small platform with surprising agility, barely jostling me in his arms. Then he's striding toward a wooden door that leads to a spiral staircase going down.

What registers first is the warmth—or perhaps the absence of the chill wind that had whipped at us outside. The gargoyle descends the steps slowly, and I peer downstairs, curious despite myself. This is what I came here to explore, after all, even if I imagined a different chain of events to get in here.

At the bottom of the stairs, another door awaits, with a sliver of yellow light coming from underneath it. The gargoyle moves me carefully in his arms and lifts the latch, then dips his head so his horns don't brush the lintel.

We enter a large space that must span almost the entire diameter of the tower. The outer wall is rounded, confirming my theory. The windows, which seemed abandoned from the outside, are actually paned with glass, the shutters closed for the night, but it's the open fireplace and the fire blazing within that captures my attention.

I let out a low moan at the thought of getting warm. Until this point, I hadn't allowed myself to think about how cold I was—I was too focused on the pain. But now a shiver goes through me, and my eyes prick with tears at the knowledge of just how close I'd come to meeting my end out there.

"Klaus?"

A male voice jerks my attention to the right. There's an armchair by the fire, a large one I hadn't even noticed because I was so intent on the heat of the flames. But in that armchair is another gargoyle, a paperback book dangling from his hand, staring at us in shock.

CHAPTER 3

MORGAN

"Um, hello." I raise a hand and wave awkwardly at the other gargoyle. "So sorry to disturb your evening."

Slowly, my thoughts are rearranging themselves, and I realize how idiotic I must look. I'd thought I could traipse around in the forest, find out the truth about the local spooky stories, and satisfy my professional curiosity. Instead, I nearly died—and now I'm crashing these guys' Christmas Eve, making trouble for them.

In my defense, I was pretty desperate to do something with my life. I couldn't go on living as I was, slowly crumbling under the weight of my student loan debt and boredom from working an unsatisfying job. I'd come to a point where I knew I'd lose everything if I didn't take control, and this was my last-ditch effort to do it.

Instead, I'd injured myself, possibly worsening my financial situation, and ruined their cozy evening.

The gargoyle carrying me speaks, but not in English this time. A rapid stream of German—and I'm eighty-five percent certain it *is* German—falls from his lips, and the other guy, who must be Emmerich, sits up straight. He glances from my savior to me and back, his dark eyebrows climbing higher and higher.

He's as handsome as the gargoyle holding me, if a little younger. In the firelight, his gray skin has a golden hue, and when his wings flare wide, I can almost see through them, the bones and veins illuminated from behind.

My fingers itch with the need to touch them, to feel the thin membranes and find out whether their wing bones are created the same as bats'. They look similar, the humerus strong to hold the majority of the wing weight, the radius elongated for a massive wingspan. Then I blink, forcing the thoughts away. Of course I can't just walk up to a supernatural creature and ask if I could feel him up.

The gargoyle stands, carefully places a bookmark in his book, and puts it on a shelf. Then he approaches slowly, something like hope in his expression. When he's close enough to touch, he inhales through his nose, his nostrils flaring.

And he smiles, his rough features creasing, turning him from merely handsome to extraordinary. Without warning, he takes my hand and holds it between his palms, patting it gently.

"Hello, human," he says. His voice holds a similar accent, though its timbre is different. "I'm very happy to meet you."

"Um." I try to shake his hand, but he's still rubbing his thumbs over my palm, so that doesn't work. "Hi, I'm Morgan. Morgan Grabowski."

"And I am Emmerich Bauer," he tells me. "You are very beautiful."

The gargoyle carrying me snaps something at him in

German, then twists away so my hand is yanked from Emmerich's grip. He carries me to the armchair and gently deposits me in it, then pulls up a chair so I can rest my injured leg on it.

"This is Klaus Mertz, my roost mate." Emmerich pops up beside me. "He says he found you in the forest. Does your leg hurt very badly?"

I shuffle around and take my backpack off, bringing it into my lap. I clutch it to my chest, suddenly unsure of myself. They're both looming over me, tall and imposing, and I don't know what to do.

Emmerich sniffs the air again, then lets out a sound of dismay. He crouches in front of me and takes my hand again. "Don't be afraid, human Morgan. You are safe here."

He sounds so earnest, I can't help but relax a little. If they meant to hurt me, they could do so easily, but they're just staring at me. Klaus hovers awkwardly by the fire while Emmerich pats my hand.

"I'm sorry," I say. "I only…"

I stop myself because how can I explain that I came here to research them? I wasn't sure what I was going to find, but I wasn't counting on sentient creatures with a cozy, book-filled apartment in this decrepit tower. I thought they'd be more like bats, wary of me but content to let me study them from a distance.

This is completely different.

"So…" I push my damp hair behind my ear with my free hand. "You're gargoyles?"

Klaus says something in German, and Emmerich laughs, his wings flaring out on both sides.

"Did you really think he was a demon?" he demands, turning to me. "I must tell all our friends about this, they will tease him."

My cheeks heat with a flush. "I've never met a gargoyle

before. I'm sorry if I insulted you," I say to Klaus, "but you surprised me. You had the horns and the wings…"

I shrug helplessly, my words trailing off.

"And the tail." Emmerich whips his long tail through the air behind him. He chuckles. "But we are not demons, no. Gargoyles are protectors, human Morgan."

"Just Morgan is fine," I say, smiling despite myself.

He's adorable, like an eager puppy—if puppies were almost seven feet tall and armed with deadly claws and super strength.

"What do you mean, you're protectors?" I ask.

But before Emmerich can reply, Klaus steps closer, interrupting us. "You're wet. You need to get warm so I can take you to the hospital."

"Oh!" Emmerich jumps up, unfolding his big body. "You've been hurt! Let me see."

He goes as if to touch my boot, and I flinch back instinctively, afraid he'll hurt me with his big hands. He stops, looking crestfallen at my retreat.

"I-I'll take my boot off," I say. "It's just—it hurts a lot."

Emmerich nods, his expression serious. "I'm sorry. I didn't think of that."

I ease off my boot, gritting my teeth at the pain. The swelling makes my task more difficult, and by the time I manage to pry off my damp sock, I'm crying, tears rolling down my cheeks. Emmerich crouches beside me again, murmuring something in German that sounds like he's trying to soothe me, and for some reason, it works. I give him a wobbly smile and swipe my palms over my cheeks, then focus on my foot.

The ankle is swollen, that's for sure, but it doesn't look deformed or too bruised. It hurts to the touch, but after I leave it alone for a couple of minutes, the throbbing pain lessens to an ache. If I'm lucky, it's only sprained, so I'll just have to rest and ice it, but if it gets any worse by tomorrow, I'll have to go to the ER and get an X-ray done.

"Here." Klaus appears beside me, holding out a thick blanket. "Your parka is all damp."

I accept his offer and shuck off my outer layer. The two gargoyles watch me maneuver in the armchair, and Emmerich jumps in to steady me while I shove off my snow pants. Then I collapse back, dressed in thermal leggings and my fleece sweater, breathing hard.

A moment passes as we all stare at each other. Their attention is unwavering, and when they focus like this, they go completely still, more statue-like than ever.

Then Klaus clears his throat. "I can hang these for you. To dry."

I hand him my parka and snow pants, wondering how to proceed now. Him hanging up my clothes means he expects me to wait for them to dry, right? Or will he roll me up like a burrito in that blanket he brought me and fly me home?

"How is your leg?" Emmerich asks. "Do you need a human doctor?"

I bite my lip to hide a smile. What kind of doctor does he think I could need? But he seems genuinely worried about me, and for some reason, I want to put him at ease.

"It's probably just a sprained ankle. Do you have any ice, maybe?"

I glance around for the first time, taking in the space around me. There's a nook that looks like it might be a kitchen, but there's no stove, just a small counter. The place has electricity, as evidenced by a mood lamp by the bookcase, and there is a tap in the kitchen, which must mean they have running water at the very least. I wonder how they managed to put in all these amenities while the human population of Clearwater still thought this tower was abandoned.

Klaus murmurs something to Emmerich in German, then

disappears through the door we came in earlier. Emmerich drapes another blanket around my shoulders, pats my back, and bodily pushes the huge armchair—with me in it—closer to the fire. Finally, he stalks to the kitchenette and rummages around the cupboards, then brings me a small pot of what looks like chutney. I uncap it and sniff it carefully. The scent of honey and herbs wafts up at me, pleasant enough—but what am I supposed to do with it?

"Oh, good thinking," Klaus says. He returns inside and shakes snowflakes from his wings. "Here, I brought you some snow."

He hands over a large snowball, and I'm left holding the honey chutney in one hand, the snowball in the other.

"Um." I glance from Klaus to Emmerich. "Thanks?"

Emmerich crouches by my feet. "You put the salve on the ankle," he says slowly. "Irma said it would work on us, so there's reason to believe it will do for you, too."

"It's medicinal?" I sniff at it again, wondering who Irma is. "I thought you brought me a snack."

Klaus looks horrified. "No, no, it's spelled. Not a good idea to eat it, definitely not for humans."

"Right." I hold out the snowball to Emmerich. "Do you have a towel I could wrap this in? It'll hurt if I put it directly on my skin."

He seems confused for a moment, then shrugs and goes to fetch the towel. I scoop up some of the salve and hesitate for a moment. I don't have any cuts on my skin, so at least I can be reasonably sure the salve won't cause an infection, but is it smart to put *spelled* goop on my leg?

Only one way to find out.

Under Klaus' watchful eye, I smear it on. A light tingle spreads from it, sort of like a soothing balm, but the longer it rests, the deeper it penetrates, spreading a cooling sensation through my aching ankle.

"Ohhh." I inspect my injury. It doesn't look any different, but it definitely feels better. "This is some good stuff."

"I forgot we had it," Klaus admits. "Emmerich is the one who bought it from the magical apothecary."

I blink up at him. "The magical apothecary?"

He cocks his head to the side. "The one next to the bakery in town."

My thoughts spin as I try to come to terms with this. I knew Arielle had discovered some strange dating app that allows you to be matched with a monster, and I heard the rumors about the supernatural presence in town. But I've visited the pharmacy next to the bakery several times for my pill prescription and just general over-the-counter meds resupply after moving, and I had no idea it was actually an *apothecary*.

Emmerich bustles up with the snow wrapped in a clean kitchen towel. "Will this do?"

"Yeah, that's perfect."

I ease the cool bundle onto my ankle and pat it down. Then I'm all done, with my injury taken care of and nothing more to do, yet the two gargoyles are still standing there, staring at me.

Heat rises in my cheeks, and I think of how I must look, in my sports clothes, with mussed hair and chapped lips, tired after a long day.

"I didn't mean to impose," I say quietly. "I'm sorry for upsetting your evening."

Emmerich crowds closer and takes my hand again. He keeps touching me at every opportunity, and I don't hate it. His energy is so pure, I don't feel uncomfortable with him at all.

"You didn't upset us," he says. Then he glances at Klaus and says something in German again, words that have Klaus growling at him.

A jolt goes through me at the sound. He looks fierce, his eyebrows drawn together, a muscle ticking in his jaw. I remember at once that I'm in the presence of monsters, so I draw my hand away from Emmerich and scoot as far as the armchair will allow.

Emmerich turns his attention on me once more, his gray-blue eyes wide. "No, don't be afraid, Morgan. What's the matter?"

I swallow past a suddenly tight throat. "I don't know. But he seems angry, and if you're speaking German, I can't understand you." I think the reality of my situation has finally caught up with me, now that the adrenaline is wearing off. "You offered to take me home. We can do that. I don't want to overstay my welcome."

The truth is, I'm alone with two strange men, and no matter how kind they are, they're still monsters. I don't know enough about gargoyles to know what could have made Klaus scowl like that. I don't want to leave before I've had a chance to learn more about them, but maybe I could return another day, when I'm better, or meet with them in a different location, closer to town.

"No more German," Emmerich blurts immediately. "I'm sorry. I didn't think about how that would make you feel."

Klaus nods, too, though his forehead is still creased in a frown, an aura of menace surrounding him.

"What did you say?" I ask the younger gargoyle. "To make him this angry?"

Klaus finally lets out a breath and drags his big palm over his face. "Forgive me. He suggested we should bring in a healer, a witch we know in town. Irma doesn't make house calls, but he does. That did not sit well with me, but I didn't want to frighten you."

I stare up at him, confused. "Why would that make you angry? Would the witch want to hurt me?"

Emmerich shakes his head, grinning. "Oh, no. Donovan is very kind. But he is male."

It takes me a moment to understand.

"And that bothers you?" I ask Klaus. "The thought of another man taking care of me?"

His throat bobs as he swallows. Then he gives me one curt, decisive nod.

"Why?"

It's a simple question, but I need the answer—and if I so much as think that he's lying to me, I'll demand to be taken away from here immediately.

Klaus lets out another low growl, his fists clenched so tight, his gray knuckles turn pale. Then Emmerich nudges him with his elbow, his expression almost imploring.

"Because you are our roost mate, Morgan," Klaus says. "And I cannot bear the thought of letting another man close to you until we're fully mated."

CHAPTER 4

KLAUS

We've fucked up. The most beautiful woman I've ever seen is staring up at me like I'm nothing but a beast, a feral creature she needs to escape from. The scent of her fear still teases my nostrils, and it kills me to know that I'm the one who triggered that reaction in her.

"Klaus," Emmerich murmurs, his voice soothing. "We don't have to bring the healer here."

I can't even look at him. *I'm* the one screwing this up, and my roost mate, the male who followed me here from our homeland, who trusted me to complete our roost, might end up losing this opportunity because of me.

He will never forgive me if I drive Morgan away.

So I turn my back on them both, leaving him to take care of her until I can calm down and get a hold of my emotions. I've just been dreaming about finding our final roost mate for *so long*, and now Emmerich is suggesting we bring another man here? Before I've had a chance to claim Morgan and mark her as mine in all the ways?

I stalk out of the room and up to the roof. Maybe the cold air will clear my thoughts—or maybe I'll remain up here all night, guarding our tower from above.

From what threat, I don't know—it's just that my instincts are driving me to make sure that my mates, both of them, are protected. If I can't touch Morgan, I better stay as far away from her as possible while still ensuring her safety.

Cold snowflakes drift from the night sky as I stand on the roof, turning my face up. Morgan had said that the snow would hurt her if she put it on her soft human skin. What a joke the Fates are playing on us. We are some of the roughest creatures in the world, born of stone if the legends of our creation are to be believed, and yet Emmerich and I have been mated to a woman who felt so light in my arms. She'd nearly died from the cold and injured her leg just walking through the forest.

What if I hurt her?

I barely touched her, and I already knew that I couldn't squeeze her too hard, or she'd have bruises all over. One careless move, and I could break her bones—and how were we supposed to mate without touching? And if I bit her…

A flash of heat goes through me as I remember the weeks after I first met Emmerich. We'd taken one sniff at each other and *knew*. Gargoyles fuck hard enough that humans in the old country made up stories about how we bring on thunder and lightning. The moment I laid eyes on Emmerich, I'd wanted to slam him against a wall and fuck him senseless—and I did. I gave him a mating bite that same day, driving him wild with passion. Then he'd thrown *me* around, giving as good as he got, and we'd spent days locked together, fucking with abandon.

Now our third mate is a soft, breakable human. I

wanted to fuck her while flying with her earlier, but she'd been hurt and cold, and the mere thought of shoving my dick inside her body had me feeling like a monster. What kind of a mate will I be to her if I can't curb those impulses? If I overstep and take things from her she isn't prepared to give?

A door closes in the stairwell below, but I don't turn around. The heavy footsteps tell me it's Emmerich who's drawing closer—of course, it can't be Morgan. She's resting, her ankle too sore to walk.

He stops beside me, staring out into the forest. He's silent for a moment, his hot breaths steaming in the frigid air. Then he puts his arms around my waist, slowly embracing me.

"You found her," he rasps in German. "Thank you."

I let out a low growl. "And look how it's going. She's so scared of me, we'll lose her before we ever really had her."

He pulls back, shaking his head. "We won't. She is curious, and if we play this right, that will change to something more soon." He pats my cheek. "I asked her again if she wanted me to take her to a human doctor, and she refused. She wants to remain here, Klaus. She's human, but she must feel the force of the bond as well."

I lift my gaze, fighting the insidious hope that flares in my chest. "You really think so?"

He grins, his handsome face radiating joy. "Oh, yes. I will fly to Jasper's house now. He will have blankets and food fit for humans."

Before I can stop him, he launches himself off the roof, his broad wings snapping wide as he catches a current of air.

"Emmerich, wait," I call after him, wanting to demand why the hell he'd need to ask our kraken friend for help.

But the wind snatches my voice away, and Emmerich disappears in a flurry of snow, leaving me standing alone on the rooftop.

With our human mate just a flight of steps away, probably waiting for him to return.

"*Scheiße.*"

I scrub my palms over my face, wiping away the accumulating snowflakes. I have a choice to make. Surely Emmerich told Morgan that he was leaving—that means she'll wait downstairs, right? I could just wait here for Emmerich's return.

But the thought of her hurt and alone won't let me remain here. Cursing under my breath, I stomp down the stairs and into our living quarters, expecting to find Morgan glaring at me, or perhaps cowering in fear.

Instead, our mate is collapsed in the armchair, head leaning back, her mouth parted in sleep. Her glasses have slipped down her nose a little. A twist of longing goes through me, wild and painful, and I can't stop my feet from carrying me closer.

Her blanket has fallen off her shoulders, so I tuck it around her safely. Her injured ankle still rests on the chair, the wrapped snow melting slowly, wetting the hem of her tight leggings. I greedily follow a droplet of water that slides down her pale skin, wishing I could trace it with my tongue.

When she'd removed her outer clothing earlier, she'd revealed her tall, curvy form that had been hidden under layers of waterproof fabric. She'd looked rather shapeless when I'd found her in the snow, but I hadn't cared one bit—I saw her beautiful eyes and scented her, and that had been enough for me.

But to discover that our mate's tits are so full and perfect, to imagine how her strong thighs would wrap around my waist…

I jerk my hand away from her, moving back. I was reaching out almost unconsciously, drawn to her. But when she was awake earlier, she'd looked at me in fear, so I can't touch her now. If she woke and shied away from me, that would be too painful.

So I settle in a crouch beside her, watching over her as she sleeps. The ordeal of trudging through snow with an injured ankle and the fright she got when she saw me must have been too much for her. I don't know how to act with her. If I behave like I normally do, will she get even more frightened and leave? She didn't seem afraid of Emmerich, even though he was his usual self, but he's softer than me. Kinder.

She stirs in her sleep, her head lolling to the side. I glare at her for a moment, then shuffle closer. Her neck will hurt if she stays in this position for too long. Even I know that, and I'm a gargoyle, not a weak human.

Not weak.

My mind corrects me immediately, some instinct admonishing me fiercely. Morgan isn't a weakling, despite her softness and the injury she sustained. I spied on her through the branches, circling overhead when I noticed a shape moving through the forest, and saw how bravely she fought to keep herself from freezing.

All right, she's not weak, but that doesn't mean I want to just leave her like this if I can help it. If I don't, she'll be in even more pain, and that's not something I can allow.

Careful not to prick her with my claws, I cup her face with my hand and gently support her head.

Morgan sighs, her warm breath fanning over my skin. I shiver, barely holding back a groan. She's so damn close, so warm, and I can't have her. My cock has been half hard since the moment I scented her, but humans are different than gargoyles. If she was one of us, she'd be just as insatiable, hungry for her mates. But with her, we have to move slowly, carefully. I will have to talk to Emmerich and make him aware of this. He's too eager, and I don't want him to scare her off.

My mate shifts in the armchair, and with that small movement, her leg slips off the chair. It thumps to the floor before I can catch it, and Morgan wakes with a yelp of pain, her pretty face scrunched up in a grimace.

"Ow!" She pulls her foot in, still sleepy, bumping it against the seat of the armchair. "Ow, shit, that hurts."

Her groan of pain sends fury through me. I would hack the armchair to pieces and burn them all if it helped her, but I shove the impulse down and take her hand instead.

"Slow down," I grumble at her, "and rest your foot back on the chair. You're hurting yourself."

She blinks at me as if she only just realized I was there. When she pushes her glasses up her nose, I recognize it as a nervous gesture, but then she does as she's told, slowly relaxing again. "How long was I out?"

I check the old clock standing on the mantelpiece. "Not long. Emmerich left less than an hour ago. You should go back to sleep. Rest will help you."

Morgan rolls her shoulders. "I don't think I could. Now that I've had my nap, I feel pretty good."

She seems rested, that's true. Her coffee-brown eyes are brighter than before, a keen intelligence shining through as she studies me, then casts her gaze around the room. I do the same, surveying the space with a critical eye. There's no clutter, which I dislike, but the room is sparsely furnished, the large couch, the wide bookcase, and the wardrobe some of the only items in sight.

"Where do you sleep?" she asks suddenly. "I just realized there's no bed here. Are there more rooms in the tower?"

The thought of Morgan in a bed is dangerous, especially since I just decided we needed to take things slowly. My cock doesn't care about that, though. It swells in my pants, throbbing with an insistent heartbeat. I shift a little so I'm hidden by the armchair and clear my throat.

"The bathroom is downstairs," I tell her. "And some storage space. Lots of empty rooms we haven't renovated yet. But this is our main living area."

"Oh." Morgan's eyebrows draw down. "So where do you sleep?"

I grin at her, because that's such a human thing to ask. "We crouch. Like so."

I shuffle back, find a comfortable crouching position, and settle my wings against my back. Then I put my fists on the floor for balance and close my eyes, showing Morgan how we sleep. I couldn't rest now if I tried—I slept for a full twenty-four hours after our last watch assignment two days ago, so I don't need it, and besides, I'm too worked up over Morgan being here.

"Wow!" Morgan's voice sounds closer suddenly. "You look exactly like a statue."

When I open my eyes, she's staring right at me, her face inches from mine. She's reaching out a hand, but when she sees me watching her, she jerks back.

"You can touch me," I rumble. "I don't mind at all."

Her eyes go wide, but she slowly brings her hand to my horn and strokes gently, running her fingers from base to tip. I bite back a groan. Our horns aren't as sensitive as Krampuses', and I barely feel her touch, but the fact that my mate has her hands on me, is touching me freely, is incredible. Emmerich will be so jealous when he returns.

The thought has me grinning. Morgan sucks in a breath and twitches, and I curse myself for a fool, immediately closing my lips.

She touched me, and I showed her my fangs. She probably thought I was about to bite her hand.

"No, do it again," she says softly, her gaze on my mouth.

I blink. "What?"

Her gaze jerks up, and a pretty flush of color spreads over her cheeks. "I liked your smile." She pulls her hand back and tucks her curly hair behind her ear. "It was the first time I saw you do it, and I just wanted to see it again. Never mind. I'm sorry, I didn't mean…"

She's babbling, embarrassed, and it's adorable, so I grin again, relief coursing through me.

She's not afraid.

My nose confirms the realization. Morgan doesn't smell scared at all. Her scent remains soft and spicy.

She stops talking and returns my smile. For the first time since I heard her shuffling in the forest, I feel hopeful. She's responding to me as a mate should, relaxing more and more. So maybe I haven't fucked everything up, after all.

Morgan settles back into the armchair after a moment and inspects her ankle. "That salve helped. It's pretty incredible. It still hurts, but I think the swelling has gone down a little, don't you?"

I hand her the pot of the ointment Emmerich found for her. "Put more on. You'll be good as new tomorrow."

She spreads the rich-smelling salve on her skin, then uses the still-cool tea towel to wrap her ankle tight. Then she looks up at me and asks, "Can you show me the bathroom, please?"

I straighten without thinking. "Of course. I'll carry you."

Morgan sucks in a breath, her eyes flaring wide. And I realize my hard cock is staring her right in the face.

CHAPTER 5

MORGAN

"*Scheiße*."

Klaus curses, whirling around to face away. His wings flare wide, his shoulders bunching up, and he stomps off until he's as far from me as he can be without leaving the room.

I remain in the armchair, clutching the pot of salve, and stare after him, because surely that couldn't have been…

"Oh my," I breathe, heat rising in my face. That was Klaus' cock I just saw, outlined perfectly by his dark pants. How long has he been hard? And is it because of me?

Earlier, before Emmerich left, Klaus had said that I was their third roost mate. I don't know what that means, exactly. Emmerich promised that they would explain everything to me once Klaus calms down, but then he'd left to gather supplies for me, as he'd put it.

Now Klaus is here, clearly aroused, and I'm…alone with him in this remote tower.

So why aren't I scared?

"I'm sorry," Klaus croaks from the other side of the room.

I glance up at him to find him looking at me over his shoulder, still angling his body to hide his state from me.

"Please, ignore what you saw," he adds. "I will not hurt you, Morgan. I could never hurt you."

He sounds so desperate, so embarrassed, my heart melts a little.

"Hey, it's all right. I'm not scared, see?" I point at myself, not knowing exactly how to signal that I'm fine. "I know it's not a voluntary reaction. You don't have to run from me."

I keep my voice soft and low, coaxing him back to my side. I don't know why this is so important, but the last thing I want is to make Klaus embarrassed and uncomfortable in his own home.

"Would it help if I…left?" I ask. "My ankle is feeling much better. If I'm making things hard for you, there's no need for me to stay."

The moment the words leave my mouth, I want to smack myself. I don't want to leave, not now that I've found them. But Klaus takes a couple of steps toward me before he stops abruptly, as if his feet carried him forward without his permission.

"No, don't leave," he rasps. "I don't want you to go."

The vehemence of his words settles something inside me. He's telling the truth. He wants me here, despite his earlier grumpiness, and for some reason, that's exactly what I needed to hear.

I relax back in the armchair and breathe out a sigh of relief. It's research, I tell myself. If I remain here, I'll find out more about the gargoyles. No scientist would pass up the chance to learn firsthand about a new species, especially one so interesting.

My stomach twists painfully at those thoughts, and guilt descends, bitter and unpleasant. Emmerich and Klaus brought me into their home, offered me shelter, and saved me from what could have been my last adventure in the woods. Emmerich has gone to fetch me food, and they've only been nice to me—so how can I think of them as research subjects? Nothing more than lab mice, creatures to be observed and studied.

I don't know what I was going to do with this knowledge before tonight. I had a vague idea of writing up a paper, taking photos of the creatures living in the tower, and becoming the first scientist to document a new species. I'd become famous, I'd be invited to conferences and symposiums all over the world to speak about this, and I'd show Andy I'm a good researcher without him. *He* certainly never discovered anything new on his own. His papers were never published in the important scientific journals, and his PhD dissertation was boring as hell.

But how can I expose Klaus and Emmerich like that?

Something sour settles in my chest, the knowledge that I'd be a terrible person if I went along with this. If I exposed their sanctuary to the world. Humans would flock to this remote, safe location, wanting to see the flying monsters. The authorities might try to seize them—study them, even.

Humans are so adept at ruining everything that smells even remotely different than their pre-conceived notion of "normal."

I can't do that to them.

With a clarity I haven't felt in ages, I know that this is *not* a path I can take and live with myself.

I take off my glasses and wipe them with the hem of my t-shirt to collect my thoughts. What does that mean for me? For us?

I don't have the answer to that question yet, and maybe I don't need it right now. Maybe it's okay to wait and see how this plays out.

Lifting my head, I find that Klaus is still gazing at me, all while keeping his body angled away. His neck must be hurting by now, but he seems intent on keeping me in his sights.

"I'd still like to go to the bathroom." I put my glasses back on and try to keep my voice as level as possible. "I don't mind your, ah, situation. I just need help getting downstairs, and I know you won't hurt me."

He remains still for so long, I'd think he has turned to stone if it wasn't for the occasional blink. Finally, he faces me, his wings unfurling. Illuminated by firelight, he's magnificent, a wonderful male specimen. I want to touch his wings, explore the membranes stretched so thin over the delicate-looking bones. I want to explore his tail, which is swishing behind him, betraying his nerves. But most of all, I wish I could walk up to him and embrace him, possibly even kiss him, and see where this attraction could lead us.

I stand on wobbly legs as Klaus walks closer to me. He's so silent, so watchful, but he offers me his hand so I can hop around the armchair and toward the door leading to the stone staircase. He supports me from the side, his arm around my shoulders, and half carries me downstairs to the bathroom.

There, he stops in front of the door and frowns at me. "Do you want me to walk you in?"

I flush at the thought. "No, I can manage." I grip the doorjamb and hop across the threshold. "But can you wait here? I'll need help getting back upstairs."

He nods solemnly, watching me until the moment I close the door between us. I shiver at the chill of the room—and swallow a yelp when my butt touches the cold toilet seat. The bathroom is lovely, recently renovated, but the gargoyles must not feel the cold as I do because the fireplace is unlit. I wish I could take a bath in the giant clawfoot bathtub on the other side of the room, but I'd probably have to heat water over the fire or something, and I'm way too tired for that.

I hop over to the sink to wash my hands and discover that the hot water tap does, in fact, produce hot water. The tower looks so medieval, but the gargoyles must have had plumbing installed, as well as other amenities, only they'd hidden them in clever ways, keeping the old-fashioned vibe of the fortress intact.

I want to explore every room in this place. Not just because any scientist worth her salt would do so—I'd already come to terms with the fact that this does not count as research for my paper—but because I want to know what kind of home Klaus and Emmerich have made for themselves. Do they spend all their time in the room upstairs? What do they do to pass the time if they don't have a TV or any modern electronics?

A flush goes through me at the thought of how they might occupy themselves. It was clear earlier that they're very close—that they're roost mates, whatever that means. And they seem to think that I'm one of them as well.

I'll have to ask them to explain. I hobble to the door. Maybe I could get Klaus to tell me now that he's alone. If not, Emmerich seems more easygoing, so I'll question him once he returns.

I swing the door open to find Klaus pacing on the staircase landing. He jerks his head up, and his wing brushes the wall at the movement, leaving a gash in the dark-gray stone.

I stare at it, confused, then pitch forward, reaching for Klaus' wing. "Do you have claws on your wingtips?" I demand, feeling along the outer edge of the limb. "Oh, wow, you do. That's *so* cool."

Klaus freezes beside me, his shoulders snapping back, but he doesn't pull his wing away, so I run my finger carefully over the wicked claw that scratched the wall. It's as long as my thumb and looks razor-sharp at the tip, so I take care not to prick my skin on it. Then, encouraged by how he leans into me, I run a palm over the smooth, leathery membrane of his wing. It's warm and supple, now that the wing is half folded, and much thicker than a bat's. It must be, to support Klaus' weight. It would snap tight once extended. I trace the thin finger bones one by one, noting the spiderweb of veins running through it all.

A ragged groan has me snapping my gaze up at Klaus.

"I'm sorry." I jerk my palm away. "I didn't mean…"

But he puts his arm around my waist and holds me in place. "I told you, Morgan, you can touch me anytime you want."

A flush heats my skin. "Okay, but I didn't ask…does it feel good to have your wings touched? Is it like touching an arm or a leg, or are they more sensitive?"

Klaus releases my waist and takes my hand in both of his. He flips it palm side up and rubs my skin with his thumbs. "It feels similar to this," he murmurs. "The wings are very sensitive because we need them to sense currents of air. The smallest gust could send us plummeting to the earth."

He digs his thumbs into the fleshy part of my palm, and I gasp, startled at how good that feels. I've held hands with men before, of course, but I've never had anyone do *this* before…

"And it feels *very* good to have you stroke my wings," he continues, bending low over my hand.

He carefully runs his thumb over the small stretch of skin between my pointer and middle finger, lingering in the groove for a moment. My entire body throbs in response, and I lean forward instinctively, wanting *more* of this.

My forehead bumps Klaus' chin, and I look up, startled to realize how close we are, especially with him leaning down like this. He doesn't move away, though, his fingers still on my hand. His breath warms my skin, fogging up my glasses, and I'm vaguely aware that he's closing his wings around us, shielding me.

I should push away from him. He's a stranger, and an inhuman one at that. I should be afraid, not turned on.

But my body wants this, and for once, I don't want to deny myself. So I tip my chin up, offering my mouth to Klaus.

He hesitates for a moment, his gaze flitting from my eyes to my lips and back, then closes the distance between us. His firm lips move over mine, and my eyes flutter shut at the pressure. I clutch his hand and place my other palm on his chest, feeling the warm, leathery skin under my fingertips.

Klaus' first kiss is all sweetness and restraint, his lips remaining closed. But when I slide my hand to the back of his neck and go on my tiptoes to get closer to him, he must sense my eagerness, because he puts one arm around me and tugs me closer, then darts his tongue out to lick my lower lip.

I open for him, gasping at the contact. His tongue is rougher than mine and longer, and strokes so deliciously over my lips, then dips into my mouth. A shiver goes through me at the contact. I mewl with pleasure, trying to get closer to him.

Klaus lets out a low chuckle that goes straight to my core, a sound of male satisfaction so sexy, I want to roll around in it. He pulls me flush with his chest, and I gasp at the feel of his cock nudging my belly. Fuck, it's as large as I thought. I've been trying not to stare at it since he seemed so uncomfortable earlier, but there's no hint of hesitation left in him when he rolls his hips lightly, pressing us closer together.

"Klaus," I murmur.

He nuzzles my neck, his rough tongue licking my skin. "Yes, *Engel*?"

Did he just call me an angel? I melt in his embrace, then

run my fingers into his long, dark hair. It's silky under my touch, and I tug on the strands, needing him to kiss me again.

He growls, a deep, menacing sound, but if he meant for it to intimidate me, he missed the mark completely—the vibration in his chest rolls through my body, setting all my nerve endings on fire.

I tug his head down until he kisses me again, then luxuriate in how skilled he is at driving me wild. He clutches my waist with both hands and lifts me off my feet, holding me right where he wants me, and I whimper with need, chasing contact with his lips.

I'm about to hoist myself up and put my legs around his waist when a clatter from the staircase above us captures my attention. Heavy footsteps descending signal Emmerich's return—he stops at the door to the main living area and opens the door.

"Oh God," I whisper, embarrassment surging through me. "Klaus, put me down."

"Klaus?" Emmerich calls from above. "Morgan?"

Klaus grumbles a little, then sets me on my feet, but he doesn't let me go. He doesn't open his wings either, so I can't see anything but him—his handsome face, his chest, and his large wings.

"Down here," I call. My voice comes out as a squeak, so I clear my throat and try again. "We're down here, Emmerich."

Footsteps descend again, and I sense more than see Emmerich emerging from around the bend in the central spiral staircase.

"Hello," he says from somewhere behind the gargoyle currently hiding me. "Where have you put our human, Klaus?"

Slowly, Klaus lowers his wings, then folds them back. He releases my waist and steps away from me, and I have to fight the urge to follow him because I miss the warmth of his hands. Instead, I push my glasses up my nose as if that will calm my stuttering heartbeat and face Emmerich, who's descending the stairs.

"Hello, Morgan," he says, a huge grin on his handsome face. "Has Klaus been treating you well?"

Before I can give him an answer, he drops the duffle bag he's brought with him at his feet, comes right up to me, and takes my hand. He lifts my fingers to his lips and kisses my knuckles like a gentleman, then ruins the illusion of refinement by leaning close and huffing at my neck.

"Oh, Morgan." He groans and crowds me up against the wall, leaning his big body over mine. "You smelled so good before, but now that Klaus has put his scent all over you, I want to lick you."

"Emmerich!" Klaus grabs his friend by the shoulder and tugs him back. "Give her a moment to breathe. You're scaring her."

He's wrong. I'm not scared, but I am overwhelmed—both by what happened with Klaus just moments ago and by Emmerich's imposing presence. He smells of wind and snow, and yet warmth radiates from him, delicious and inviting.

"I'm fine," I hurry to say as Emmerich's expression falls. "I'm not afraid."

Klaus harrumphs, but Emmerich seems relieved, if still a little wary.

"Forgive me," he says. "It's only that it was difficult being away from you. We haven't mated yet, so it was very hard to make myself fly away from you."

"Thank you," I blurt out. "For thinking of me."

I flush at the thought of mating. What does that entail, exactly? The simplest answer presents itself, of course, but I can't help but feel that there's more to this thing.

"Did you bring her food?" Klaus picks up the duffle bag and hefts it in one hand. "What did Jasper say?"

Emmerich takes my hand again and helps me climb the stairs, supporting me until we reach the warmth of the living room. I was so cozy in Klaus' embrace that I forgot all about the cold in that drafty stairway, and now the heat of the fire proves almost too much. Flushing from the warmth, I hobble over to the armchair and draw my fleece sweater over my head, not wanting to sweat through the thing.

A groan has me looking up. Both Klaus and Emmerich are staring at me, their expressions mirroring each other. I don't know which one of them let out that groan, but it's clear that they're…captivated. By me and my simple stretchy undershirt, a plain black one with short sleeves that I've had for years.

Emmerich recovers first, clearing his throat and reaching for the bag Klaus is still clutching in his fist. He sets it on the chair in front of me and undoes the zipper.

"Jasper has found a human mate as well," he informs Klaus, glancing at his roost mate over his shoulder. "Human Arielle has packed things for you, things she said that you'll need to stay in our drafty old tower."

I stare at the gargoyle in shock. "Arielle? You're sure that was her name?"

He glances up from rooting through what looks like a bundle of blankets and towels. "Yes, I'm certain. She introduced herself. And she smelled like Jasper, you know. He must be going into heat, judging from how strongly the house smelled of sex."

I laugh, then reach into my pocket for my phone, only to remember it's still in my jacket, hung out to dry. "Arielle is my friend," I tell them. "Klaus, could you get me my phone? I've been trying to reach her to check in but couldn't get a good signal. She went on a date, and it seems like it's going well."

Klaus wordlessly hands me my phone, but it's dead, the battery finally run out. I sigh, trying to remember what Arielle had told me about her upcoming date. She'd texted me the guy's address and then checked in as we'd agreed, but she certainly hadn't mentioned anything about finding a mate.

"What is Jasper?" I ask carefully. "Is he also a gargoyle?"

Emmerich pulls a jar of peanut butter from the duffle bag and hands it to me triumphantly, as if it's a precious treasure. "No, he's a kraken. Lots of tentacles."

Clutching the jar, I try to suppress a shudder and fail. "Tentacles?"

Klaus sends me a knowing smirk. "You prefer your men less slimy, do you?"

"I'm willing to try anything once." I squint up at him. "I won't say that tentacles are an immediate turn-on, but maybe?"

At that, he growls again, the sound more menacing than before. "You will not be trying any tentacles."

Oh. Well, then.

"How can you be so certain?" I ask earnestly.

Klaus looms over me, so I have to crane my neck to look him in the eyes. He radiates barely leashed fury, and I remember what he said earlier about not letting that healer near me.

"Hey." I take his clenched fist and pry his fingers apart until I can press my thumbs into his palm like he did for me earlier. "I'm not going anywhere. And I really don't want anyone with tentacles. But whatever is going on here is…a lot. And I don't understand."

He lets out a shuddering breath, then pulls his hand gently from my grip. He turns and stalks away, and I think for a moment that he's gone off to sulk again, but he simply picks up another chair and brings it closer to the fire. He takes a piece of firewood from a basket and throws the log onto the fire, sending sparks flying into the chimney. Emmerich puts the duffle bag on the floor and takes the other chair, his elbows on his knees.

"We do owe you an explanation," Klaus says, his voice still rough. "And I owe you an apology for behaving like this."

CHAPTER 6

EMMERICH

I stare at Klaus, worry gnawing at me. He is riding the edge of his anger, the mating instinct forcing out all the fears he's been harboring for years but never dealt with. Ever since we moved to America, he's been trying to find our remaining roost mate, and he—*we*—failed time and time again.

Now Morgan is here, and he's worried he will scare her away, and that, in turn, is making him even scarier than he usually is.

Our human mate is not a timid bunny. She was afraid at first but she is curious now more than anything, so all I need to do is calm Klaus down before he says something he might regret.

Like telling the woman of our dreams that she will *not* be fucking a kraken in the future. That she will not be fucking anyone else but us. I don't think human women appreciate orders. If Morgan was a gargoyle, she might have bitten Klaus for an outrageous statement like that. Morgan hasn't shown any inclination that she might want to bite us, but you never know with humans. They are unpredictable and strange, so maybe…

"Emmerich," Klaus snaps. "What are you doing?"

I blink and glance up at him, confused. "What?"

"You're scaring Morgan."

I whip my gaze to our mate to find her staring at me, wide-eyed.

"I'm sorry," I blurt. "I was only looking at your teeth."

"My teeth?" Morgan brings a hand up to cover her mouth. "Why?"

Klaus groans and goes to turn away from me, but I snag his hand and pull him back. I give his fingers a quick squeeze to let him know we're in this together. Whatever happens with Morgan will affect both of us, and I won't do anything to push her away.

At least not knowingly.

I release Klaus' hand and slowly reach forward, tugging on Morgan's wrist until she shows me her mouth again. Then I cup her cheek gently and run the pad of my thumb over her full lower lip. She sucks in a breath but doesn't flinch away from me, and some of my worry dissipates.

"I was trying to judge how much it would hurt Klaus if you bit him with your blunt human teeth," I explain, unable to let go of her now that I've felt her soft skin.

Morgan's straight eyebrows draw together in a frown. "Why would I bite him?"

Klaus shifts in his seat, his wings flaring out for a moment before he catches himself and tucks them tight against his back. Oh, he must like this despite himself. He's leaning forward, waiting for my answer, and I stifle a grin, knowing I have redirected his fussing into curiosity. He has a thing for biting, and if Morgan does, too, that will make things easier.

"Because he's being such a terrible brute." I grin at

Morgan, then add, "All without telling you he wants to kiss you again."

Morgan's cheeks flush prettily, and she draws away from me and pushes her glasses up her nose. It's a nervous tell of hers, I've noticed.

"Y-you know we kissed?" she breathes. "That doesn't bother you?"

I lean back and cross my arms over my chest. "Why would it? I kissed Klaus today, too. Does that bother you?"

"Of course not," she says quickly, back snapping straight. "But you two are a couple—I mean, roost mates."

"Yes," I agree. "And now you are one, too."

She matches my position, leaning back against the armchair and crossing her arms. "Explain."

I can't help but grin at her bossy command. I like her like this—and I think this is her usual demeanor, when she's not injured and frightened by big winged monsters such as Klaus.

The winged monster next to me leans forward. "We scented you and knew. You're the one we've been waiting for all this time."

Morgan's frown deepens. "No pressure," she mutters. "That doesn't explain what you expect of me."

Klaus opens his mouth again, no doubt to list all the things mates do together—fuck, bite, hunt, rest, fuck, and so on—but I don't think that will work with Morgan. She didn't know we existed up until tonight, and she needs to be eased into this.

I snap my right wing out and smack Klaus in the side with it. I might prick him with my claw a little, too, but his skin is thick, and he needs the reminder that he should tread carefully.

"Gargoyles mate for life," I tell Morgan, speaking quickly so Klaus won't speak instead of me. "Klaus and I met years ago in Germany, but we felt we needed to cross the ocean to find our mate. We've been searching far and wide."

Morgan's frown eases a little, and she listens to me intently, as if she doesn't want to miss a word.

"If you were a gargoyle, you would have felt the pull as well, a certainty right here." I place a hand over my heart, where a soft warm glow has been growing for the past hours, ever since I laid eyes on the snowy bundle in Klaus' arms. "And we would be fucking already, unable to hold back."

"Emmerich," Klaus snaps, annoyance clear in his tone.

But Morgan flaps a hand at him, impatient. "No, no, this is good. Keep going. So you have an instinct to, ah, mate immediately? Is it to continue the species?"

I blink at the question. "Er, I suppose? I would love to put a baby in you, yes."

Her cheeks flush a deeper pink, while Klaus groans at my side, burying his face in his hands.

"It might be a little too soon for babies," Morgan says, her voice higher than before. "But I understand the mating urge. It's similar in many species. I've just never heard of a bond that forms so fast." She flicks her gaze from me to Klaus and back. "And you've never experienced this with any other woman? You've met females of your kind, yes?"

Klaus lowers his hands and stares at her. "Of course we have. Not one of them was right for us."

"But you are," I add, grinning again. "You smell exactly right. And you are strong, you'll be able to bear gargoyle babies."

Now her eyes go round. "Gargoyle babies? Do they—oh God, are they *born* with wings? With horns?"

Now her scent is spiking with anxiety again, and I draw back, not understanding where I fucked up.

Klaus glares at me, then reaches forward to put a hand on Morgan's knee. "No," he says, his deep voice ringing true.

"That would make childbirth very dangerous. The wings are only small nubs at birth, as are the horns, so they don't hurt the mother."

"The tail is there from the start," I add, trying to be helpful. I swish my tail up to show Morgan. "It's not as big as this. Just a small thing, no larger than my little finger."

Morgan's breaths are coming faster now, her scent going haywire. Klaus growls, no doubt thrown into a frenzy by our mate's fear. I know she's in no danger, but seeing her so upset is wreaking havoc on my senses, too, so I stumble from my chair, kneeling in front of Morgan.

"Don't leave," I rasp. "Please, don't leave us. I'm sorry I upset you, *Liebchen*. I didn't want that. But if you're scared of me, *I'll* leave. Just don't go."

Klaus stands, no doubt to pull me off her, but I can't move, not until she sends me away. I won't leave my mate willingly, but if Morgan decides she doesn't want me here, I won't stay. I couldn't live with myself if I made her uncomfortable.

Morgan sits still for a moment, then a warm hand touches my shoulder. She draws in a deep inhale, then tightens her hold on me, her fingers trembling. Hope springs up in my chest, painfully bright, so I lift my head to look at her.

"I don't want you to leave," she says softly. "This is your home."

I lean my head to the side to nuzzle against her wrist. Morgan allows it, her only reaction a slight hitch in her breathing.

"You want to have babies with me?" she asks, her brown eyes still so wide.

A terrifying possibility pops up in my mind. Surely that's not... But Morgan is human, so...

"You don't want gargoyle children," I say, my voice

strangely hollow. "You kissed Klaus to see what it was like to kiss a monster, but you want your children to be pink and soft, without horns and tails and wings."

I wouldn't mind a human child. I would have to be careful with it, because if adult humans are this easily injured, their young must be even more so, helpless, pink little beans. But I wouldn't reject one, and I would care for it as best I could, even if it could never fly with me in the night sky.

I'd always imagined myself as a father, taking our children out to fly for the first time. Young gargoyles learn to fly at about three years of age, after they've toddled around the roost for a while, learned to perch and hop and exercise their wings. I'd hoped we could build a nest for them here, a comfortable nook filled with pillows and perches and blankets for them to remain cozy while their skin hardened to be like ours, near-impenetrable and thick.

We even bought the supplies to build a nest, months ago, because we'd been so hopeful. We wanted to be ready for our mate in case we met her unexpectedly.

Now we have—and she's disgusted with the thought of bearing a gargoyle child.

Morgan's fingers tremble on my shoulder, and she pulls her hand away. Her eyes fill with tears. She blinks rapidly, but they spill down her cheeks, where she dashes them away with her hand as if angry with herself for crying.

My heart hurts at the sight. It feels like it's being rent in two, both by the realization that Morgan might not want a future with us, and by her tears—which I caused.

I push to my feet and step back, not wanting to crowd her. She was so soft and willing in my arms earlier, I didn't even think that this might be a problem, but of course it is. I turn away, both to give her space and to hide the devastating disappointment coursing through me. Klaus tries to stop me, but I twist away from his hand, breaths coming faster and faster.

"I don't even *know* you," Morgan bursts out suddenly.

I whirl around to face her, and there she is, standing, one hand on the back of the armchair for support, glaring at me fiercely.

"How could I possibly know if I want gargoyle children if I've never seen one?" she demands. "I didn't even know gargoyles existed until today. Do you know human women can *die* in childbirth? My question was completely legitimate, and if that's a problem for you, I'll ask you to fly me home right now."

I blink. I have no idea what to say, because she is right. My eagerness got the better of me, and I put her in an impossible situation, asking too much of her.

She is not a gargoyle.

Humans have hunted us in the past, but I thought things might be changing at last. When I saw Jasper and his human, Arielle, earlier tonight, I knew immediately they were perfect together. Arielle didn't seem to mind the fact that her baby would eventually have tentacles, so I thought Morgan would be equally eager to mate with us.

But Morgan didn't come here to be our mate.

I want to kneel at her feet again and beg for forgiveness, but there is *something* that's been nagging me, a question I couldn't quite pinpoint—until now.

I squash down the instinct that's telling me to protect my mate, even from myself, and ask, "Why are you here?"

CHAPTER 7

MORGAN

My heart's beating too fast, my breaths coming in choppy and shallow.

"What?" I ask, merely to buy myself some time, to be able to *think*.

Emmerich, who looked so fucking *disappointed* with me just moments ago, now steps closer, his eyes narrowing in suspicion. "Why were you in the forest on our land during a snowstorm? If humans are so sensitive to cold, why would you do that to yourself?"

I would expect this kind of questioning from Klaus, who seemed the more serious of the two, more intense, but it's sweet Emmerich who's questioning me.

I don't think I can lie to them. They seemed to sense my distress, and from how fiercely Klaus is frowning now, a low growl emanating from his chest, I think he's about to launch himself at Emmerich for upsetting me—but this is exactly what I didn't want. They are roost mates—a married couple, for all intents and purposes—and I'm pushing a wedge between them. If I'm right, then this mating business is forcing Klaus to be super protective of me, to the point that he might decide to eliminate the perceived threat to my safety, who just happens to be Emmerich.

"Stop," I croak, taking a step back. "Both of you, just stop."

They blink, their expressions of surprise so similar, I'd laugh if this situation wasn't so delicate. Instead, I slump back in the armchair and take a deep breath to calm myself. I'll have to tell them the truth. They deserve it, especially if it means they'll need to send me away. If they're truly convinced I'm their mate, that will hurt them, no doubt about it. Besides, Klaus saved my life, and Emmerich went out of his way to make me comfortable, so I owe them that much.

They both stand in front of me, looming like granite statues. I don't think they're aware of the effect they have on me—this is just the way they are, gargoyles in their natural environment.

"Please, sit." I crane my neck and look from one to the other. "It will be easier to talk that way."

Klaus blows out a long exhale, then takes his seat by the fire. Emmerich hesitates for a moment, then does the same, the legs of his chair scraping on the flagstone floor as he moves it closer to me. Even now, he seems drawn to my side by some strange twist of fate.

I enjoyed their attention earlier without thinking things through. It makes perfect sense that they have different expectations for a relationship than I do. We're different species, after all. It seems that for them, reproduction is the primary goal. It also brings up the issue of long-term relationships. If I'm their chosen brood mate, will they drop me and exchange me for a new one as soon as I give them children?

And am I seriously considering being a baby mama to a pair of bat-winged supernaturals?

"Emmerich has a point." Klaus breaks the awkward silence stretching between us. "Why were you in our forest tonight?"

I swallow down my anxiety. They won't hurt me, no matter what I tell them, I know that. But they might decide I'm too much trouble after all, and fly me back to town. If they were worried about me exposing them to the world, they could even leave the area, and I'd have no proof of their existence.

The thought of them leaving sends horror coursing through me. I've only just met them!

"I was searching for the haunted tower," I admit. "I heard stories about winged creatures flying around here, and I wanted to come and see what the fuss was all about."

Klaus lifts one black eyebrow. "All alone? And on Christmas Eve? Aren't humans usually busy with their families at this time of year?"

His piercing gray eyes are unflinching as he stares at me, and my stomach twists at the realization that I'll have to explain *everything* to them or risk sounding like I'm hiding something significant—something dangerous to them.

That won't do, not when my only crime is trusting a man I shouldn't have.

"I didn't have enough time or money to go visit my parents this year," I begin, my voice small. "They live near Richmond, Virginia, and I'd either have to drive down, which would be difficult in this weather, or fly, which I couldn't afford, not with the holiday ticket prices. So I told them I was spending Christmas with my friends."

My mom had been disappointed, but I *had* spent a lot of time with them recently, so she understood. And she'd been happy for me, told me how proud she was of me for picking myself up and living again.

"You lied to your parents?" Emmerich asks. "Why?"

My throat tightens painfully. "I didn't want them to worry. If they thought I was spending Christmas alone, they'd want to fly here, and Dad doesn't like flying, especially not around the holidays." I lower my gaze to my lap, unable to keep Emmerich's gaze. "And they'd see my crappy apartment, which I've been trying not to tell them about."

Klaus lets out a low, rumbling growl, then cuts it off as if it escaped without his approval. He clears his throat and asks, "Why would they be worried? And why is your apartment crappy?"

My cheeks flame at the intrusive questions, but I know he doesn't see them as such. These two are living in an old tower, sure, but they've renovated it beautifully. Every time I glance around the room, I see more signs of their impeccable taste. There are cozy cushions on the couch, thick velvet drapes on the windows, and small bookshelves built into wall niches wherever there's room. The rug in front of the couch must have cost a fortune, and the same goes for the landscape painting on the far wall, which looks like it might be some sort of a Romantic original.

I glance from Klaus to Emmerich. They were so happy earlier, thinking they'd snagged a great human mate for their roost, but in truth, I'm not exactly a catch.

I don't want to tell them the truth, but how can I keep it from them? It would be unfair, and they need to have all the facts before deciding what to do with me.

Looking down at my lap, I take a deep breath to brace myself. "My apartment is crappy because I can't afford a better one. It's close to where I work, which is at an eco-agricultural company, and it's incredibly boring, but it pays the bills. I have a lot of those," I say with a wry smile. "Before I arrived in Clearwater to take this job, I was a junior researcher on a national bat conversation project. So was my fiancé."

"Fiancé?" Klaus growls.

At the same time, Emmerich blurts, "Bat conservation?"

I nod at Emmerich. "I studied conservation biology. Bats are the most fascinating creatures, which is why I was intrigued when I heard about giant winged creatures living in an abandoned tower in the middle of the forest."

He snorts, but before he can say anything, I swing my gaze to Klaus because I need to get the story out now or I'll never finish.

"He's an ex-fiancé now. He cheated on me, and there was no way I could work with him, so I was left without a job and without an apartment because he was the one listed on our rental contract." I shrug, trying to look more casual than I actually feel. "I haven't talked to him in several months, and I'm over him in the sense that I don't miss *him* anymore. I didn't take the breakup well, though. It got pretty bad a couple of months ago when I was still living with my parents, so that's why they've been worried for me. That's why I told them I was spending the holidays with friends."

I push my glasses up my nose and add, "I've been doing online therapy for weeks now, so I'm a lot better than before, but I'm still a bit short on the friend front." I click my tongue and correct myself, "Well, no, I have Arielle, but she had other plans for Christmas, which apparently included finding a kraken boyfriend, so I didn't want to interrupt. I was going to spend the evening at home, watch TV and microwave a pineapple-ham pizza, but then I decided that was too sad for me and went out on an adventure."

I spread my arms as if to indicate that we all know how that story ended. I could have died in the forest and would have frozen if Klaus hadn't found me.

"Did you come here to expose us?" Klaus asks, his voice level.

I stare at him, wondering what his question really means. Would he get angry if I said yes? Keep me from leaving?

And would that be so bad?

"I didn't know you were...sentient," I say carefully. "I didn't even fully believe the legends were true. I thought that an especially large colony of bats might be living here, or, if the creatures people told me about really turned out to be supernatural, that they'd be..." I gesture with my hand, searching for the right words. "I don't know what I thought. But the moment I saw this place, right after you saved me, I knew I could never write a *paper* about you. I already messed up your Christmas—I'm not about to ruin your lives as well."

"You didn't ruin anything—" Emmerich starts to say, leaning forward to grasp my hand.

But Klaus cuts him off, his expression severe. "You wouldn't just be exposing us. There are dozens of supernaturals in Clearwater. You'd be putting everyone in danger, including your friend, Arielle, and her kraken boyfriend, as you said, because humans would descend on this place and tear it apart, searching for more proof of anything strange. There are *children* here, Morgan. Families who have lived here for decades, creating a safe haven for creatures like us."

My eyes well with tears at the thought of uprooting innocent people's lives. "I would *never*. Please, you have to believe me. I ditched that plan the moment I met you. I'm sorry I ever thought it was a good one at all."

"You're a scientist," Klaus replies, still frowning. "Will you be able to let this go? We are not rabbits to be studied."

"Of course not," I agree quickly. "But..." I chew on my lip, not knowing how to phrase my issue.

Klaus' gaze softens a fraction, and he leans in, taking my

other hand. "What is it? You can tell us anything. You already know our secret, Morgan."

"I'm just *curious*," I burst out, pulling my hands from theirs. "I mean, you're *gargoyles*. You talk about reproduction and mate bonds and tails and horns, and my mind is about to explode! I have so many questions. So. Many. Questions!"

I put my fingers to my temples, then spread them out, miming a head explosion.

Before either one of them can say anything, I add, "I want to measure your wingspan and test how far you can fly, I want to study your horns under a microscope to see if they're made of keratin like a goat's, and also test your resistance to cold because *how* are you both not freezing when you go out in the snow? But I know that's not going to happen because you're intelligent individuals and studying you would be *wrong*."

I say all this very fast, the words rushing from me, and only stop myself after I see their shocked expressions.

"I'm sorry," I whisper. "I, um, get carried away sometimes. I would never study you because that would make you uncomfortable. Also, it would be unethical, I'm pretty sure. And I'd never tell anyone. I swear. It's just a professional deformation, wanting to know everything."

The gargoyles both stare at me, their focus unwavering. Klaus' expression is still unreadable, his rough-hewn features stony. But Emmerich is grinning again, which has some of my tension melting away. He's hovering on the edge of his seat, and when he meets Klaus' gaze, his smile widens. I bite the inside of my cheek—it's Klaus' approval I need. Emmerich seems satisfied with my explanation, but if Klaus refuses to believe me…

The corner of Klaus' mouth tips up in a grudging smile, and he lifts one shoulder in a shrug as if to say, why not?

Emmerich lets out a long exhale, then pats my knee. "You

can study me. I'll be your subject, Morgan. Just don't cut off my horns, they take ages to grow back."

A great bubble of relief grows in my chest, expanding outward. "Y-you're serious? You're not angry?"

"We can smell you're telling the truth," Klaus confirms. "And if you *weren't* a curious scientist, who knows if our paths would have crossed."

I let out a laugh that sounds too much like a sob, and all my emotions come crashing over me. I was so afraid they'd send me away—I didn't even know how much their acceptance meant to me until this moment.

"Ach, don't cry," Emmerich says, his eyebrows furrowing. "Come here."

In a quick move, he reaches forward, grabs me by my waist, and hauls me to his lap. I flail a little, then settle in his warm embrace and lean my head on his naked chest. His leathery skin is so intriguing, I can't stop myself from running my palm over his biceps. Then I realize I'm feeling him up and drop my hands to my lap. A couple of deep breaths later, I'm calm enough to peek up at Klaus, who's been watching us in silence all this time.

"Thank you for believing me," I say softly. "And I'm sorry—"

"Stop that," Klaus commands. "No more apologies."

"Okay." I offer him a small smile. "If I ever ask too many questions or make you uncomfortable, you have to tell me."

Emmerich nods, his chin brushing my temple. "I will have lots of questions, too. Starting with this strange noise your insides are making."

I jerk in his lap. "Oh. That's my stomach rumbling. It means I'm hungry. I haven't eaten since lunch."

Klaus frowns at me. "Why didn't you say something?"

"I forgot!" I put a hand on my belly, pressing in lightly. "I was busy discovering some mythological creatures, you know."

Emmerich's chest rumbles with a laugh. "Jasper's human, Arielle, packed some food for you. But you will have to tell us when you get hungry, or we might forget to feed you."

"How many times a day do humans eat?" Klaus asks, already reaching for the duffle bag Emmerich brought back from his expedition earlier. "Do you need to eat every day?"

I blink, gaze darting from one to the other. "Um, yes, we eat every day, preferably three to five meals. I like three main ones, then some snacks to make it through the day."

Klaus stares at me in disbelief, then shakes his head. "How do humans achieve anything if they spend half their days eating?"

"I assume you don't?"

I'd noted the absence of a stove before, but I thought that maybe they preferred eating out.

"We hunt every ten days or so," Emmerich says. "The woods here are full of deer and other wild game."

It's my turn to gape at them. "You catch your own food?"

"We are very good hunters," Klaus assures me. "Usually we'll take down a deer together. That's enough to last us both for a week or more. We eat more frequently if we're flying a lot, but I can't imagine having to eat every day."

Emmerich is nodding along. "It would make sentry jobs very difficult if I was hungry all the time."

I raise my eyebrows at them. "Sentry jobs?"

"We work for a private security company," Klaus explains. "We'll often take night shifts, guarding buildings or people, depending on the assignment."

I imagine a pair of gargoyles sitting on a rooftop somewhere, so much like medieval church statues. But surely that must make things difficult if they actually have to defend their target from humans? How do they keep from getting spotted? Surely people would notice two massive statues just appearing out of nowhere?

Klaus snorts out a laugh, his serious expression lightening. "I can almost hear your head bursting with all the questions. You're wondering how we move around human society, yes?"

He roots through the duffle bag and sets a pair of apples on the now-empty armchair. He adds a jar of peanut butter, a pot of jam, and a bag of sliced bread to the collection, along with three bananas and a bottle of milk.

I give him a sheepish smile and pick up a banana. "That thought did cross my mind, yes."

"We wear glamours," Emmerich explains as he carefully unscrews the cap on the milk bottle and hands it to me. "Irma at the apothecary creates amazing charms that help us hide our wings and horns and turns our skin a human color."

"As long as we don't brush up against people or get in crowded spaces, no one notices what we are," Klaus finishes. "Now, do you want some bread? We don't have plates, but there has to be a knife somewhere…"

"That's fine," I stop him, then peer into the duffle bag. "Can I have one of those protein bars instead? That'll be enough for now."

I'm thinking of the late hour and the fact that I'll need to go to bed soon. If I eat too much right before bedtime, I'll toss and turn, my stomach too heavy to get comfortable.

"If this is how little you eat at each meal, it's no wonder you have to eat so often," Emmerich grumbles.

"Our digestive systems must be wildly different," I say between bites of banana. "Yours must be kind of like a snake's. They're known for eating a bunch of food all at once, then digesting it slowly."

"We are nothing like snakes." Emmerich lifts his chin to peer down his nose at me.

I shrug, grinning. "I'll have to research if other animals behave like that. There have to be others that you'll like better. But definitely not bats. They fly out all the time to feed on insects."

Klaus offers me a small smile. "We know. We have a colony living up in the rafters."

I nearly drop my banana at this bit of news. "You what?"

He chuckles, the sound reverberating around the room. "I thought you'd like that. There are hundreds of them, but they're hibernating for the winter. We can take you to see them tomorrow if you'd like." He offers me a sly look from under half-lowered eyelids. "That is, if you'd like to stay the night."

I finish off the last of the banana and carefully fold the peel, wondering where I should put it. "That's very devious of you, to tempt a woman with *bats*. How can I resist?"

His grin widens as he takes the peel from me and carries it into the kitchen. "Is it working?"

"Oh, yes," I call after him. "Me wanting to stay here has nothing to do with two amazing gargoyles. I'm only here for the bats."

Emmerich wraps his arms around me and squeezes me tight to his chest. "Hmm, I don't mind sharing your affection with those little critters. As long as you sleep down here and not in the cold attic."

I glance up at him. "I thought you weren't bothered by the cold."

"That doesn't mean I don't prefer this living room to that drafty old room," he grumbles. "Do you know bats poop right where they sleep? Every spring, we have to clean out all the bat shit or the ceiling would cave down on us."

"Mm, bat poop is an excellent fertilizer," I tell him. "You could sell it for some extra cash."

Klaus rejoins us, stopping in front of us, his arms crossed

over his chest. "We're not so desperate for money yet. But we'll keep that in mind."

I stretch my arms up, yawning. "What time is it? I feel like I've lived about three days' worth of adventure today, but it wasn't that late when you brought me here, was it?"

Klaus walks over to the mantel and picks up a phone. "Just past nine."

I gape at him. "You have a phone! Why didn't you— I mean, of course you have a phone, why wouldn't you? Do you—do you have a charger?"

He presses his lips together, surely to keep from laughing at my stuttering monologue, then shows me a cleverly disguised charging station on their bookshelf, with two chargers ready to use. I hop from Emmerich's lap, hobble over to where my jacket is drying by the fire, and take out my dead phone. If I manage to get a good signal, I'll let Arielle and Mrs. Rowell know I'm alive so they don't send out a search party for me. The screen lights up immediately, and I wait a minute before powering on the phone. I type out two texts and send them out, hoping they'll go through, then set the phone down, not wanting to get distracted by random emails when I have so much more interesting stuff to think about now.

I turn around to find Klaus and Emmerich both staring at me.

"What?" I ask.

Emmerich scrubs his hand over his face. "I-I like your outfit very much."

I glance down at myself, then blush. My leggings mold to my every curve, and my top has ridden up, exposing an inch of skin. Suddenly self-conscious, I tug it down again. "Thank you." The words come out as a squeak, so I clear my throat and say, "I like your style as well."

It's an understatement. Those leather pants should be

outlawed with how perfectly they outline their thick thighs and tight butts, and I have absolutely zero complaints about them going shirtless all the time.

This is dangerous territory, though. Since Klaus kissed me in the stairwell, neither of them has made a move on me—and I get that, especially since we had to discuss some really important things. But now that I should get ready for bed, I'm feeling a little awkward. They said they're okay with me kissing both of them, but how does that translate into real-life situations?

"Can I sleep on the couch?" I break the silence stretching between us. "I saw a blanket in that duffle bag, so I'm sorted for the night if that's okay with you."

Emmerich turns to Klaus. "Oh, yes, I didn't have the heart to tell Jasper and human Arielle that we have plenty of blankets for Morgan. They were being very helpful."

I frown. "You have blankets? But you said you didn't sleep…"

I trail off because Klaus is already shaking his head. He moves to the far side of the room and disappears from view behind the wall that separates this room from the spiral staircase.

"Just because we usually rest by crouching," he calls, his voice slightly muffled, "that doesn't mean we weren't prepared to nest if we found a mate."

My eyes go wide. "You-you build *nests*?"

My mind immediately conjures up a sort of giant stork's nest, a structure of branches and straw set on top of a chimney—or a tower in the middle of the forest.

Emmerich takes one look at me and grins. "What are you thinking about, *Liebchen*?"

I shake my head, not wanting to admit it. "Nothing. Will you show me?"

He steps right up to me and offers me his arm. "Yes. We'll build it just for you."

CHAPTER 8

KLAUS

All my adult life, I have been waiting for this moment. I stand in the walk-in closet Emmerich and I built when we moved here. It was one of the first things we did, before we even renovated the downstairs bathroom, because we needed a safe, dry space to store the items we brought over from Germany.

Now we'll finally get to start on the perfect nest for our mate.

For tonight, it'll have to be a simple one—enough for her to sleep in and for us to guard her. But if she decides to accept us fully, to mate with us, we'll build something more permanent.

I hope she likes it.

We didn't know who our third mate would be. If it was another male, we would have built this together and perhaps brought an adopted youngling or two into our nest to raise them as a family.

But with Morgan, we will *mate* in this nest, and if the

gods are kind and fate so inclined, we'll bring our children into the world here.

I scrub my face with my hands, suddenly overwhelmed with all the choices. Would Morgan prefer cool silks or soft cottons? Perhaps she would like fur—we haven't stored any of that for the fear of drawing in moths, but if she requested it, we would provide it.

Still, we have to start somewhere, so I take two thick mattress-like pillows made of memory foam from the lowest shelf and carry them out of the closet. We'd left room there, not too close to the fireplace, but a nice, clean space we kept scrubbed and ready. Every week when it was my turn to clean the floors, I would sweep and scrub these flagstones with a mixture of painful hope and despair at having to wait yet another day, another month for our mate.

And then she appeared all by herself, drawn in by gods know what force of nature. Her curiosity, which she apologized about several times, is the reason our roost is complete. I will answer every question Morgan will throw my way, because she wouldn't be here without her scientific, ravenous mind.

"Oh, wow," Morgan breathes as Emmerich brings her to the closet. "What is all this?"

I glance at Emmerich over her head, catching his gaze. He lifts his eyebrows as if to ask whether I want to answer Morgan's inquiry, but now that I've started building the nest, the urge to continue, and quickly, is too overwhelming to deny.

He seems to understand—he must be experiencing the same instinct. But he draws Morgan closer to his side to give me room to work and points to the mattresses I'm hauling over to the living room.

"Gargoyles build nests when mating time is near," he

explains. "We will build you a cozy nest, Morgan. You'll be so comfortable there."

"Mating time?" Morgan squeaks, her scent flaring up again.

Emmerich takes a big step away from her, his expression crushed. "Oh, no, you don't—we would never—"

I loom over Morgan in the cramped space. "This doesn't mean we have to fuck," I tell her. It's imperative that she understands this, and we can't risk driving her away. "But we do want to."

"So much," Emmerich interjects, bouncing on the balls of his feet.

I shoot him a stern glare, then focus back on our human mate. "We will do this as slowly as you like. But now that you're here, we *need* to build the nest for you. And you need somewhere to sleep."

"Oh." Morgan studies the mattresses I've already spread on the floor and hooked together with clever little clasps. "I-I'm not saying *never* on the, ah, mating point, by the way. It's just…"

Relief courses through me at her words, so I cup her cheek and trace my thumb over her soft skin. "You've been injured and you only met us today. I understand. There is no rush on any of this. But we want to make sure you're comfortable if you're willing to stay the night." I grin down at her, then add, "So you'll be able to visit the bat colony tomorrow."

Morgan returns my smile, her coffee-brown eyes lighting up. "The bats. Of course." Then she puts her hands on her hips and looks around the closet. "Okay. How can I help?"

Emmerich makes a strangled sound, which could mean he's about to pick her up and carry her straight to the nest— or he's outraged by the insinuation that we, adult gargoyles, need help building a nest from a human.

Morgan doesn't know this could be seen as an insult, though, so I grit my teeth, hoping he won't do anything too hasty.

Then my impulsive mate closes his eyes, takes a deep breath through his nose, and lets it out through his mouth. He opens his eyes and gently takes Morgan's hand. "You can tell us what pleases you," he rumbles, his voice only slightly rougher than before. "We have silk sheets, but I think humans prefer something warmer this time of year."

He draws her to the shelves and shows her the stacks of bedding we'd bought over the years, adding to our collection every time we saw a likely piece. We gathered sheets and duvets, pillows and decorative cushions, and many, many blankets.

I leave them to their exploration of the shelves and return to carrying more foam mattresses out into the living room. I don't generally care much for humans. They are a strange breed, and they have often been unkind to supernatural creatures. But they are inventive, and I'm happy Emmerich and I discovered these mattresses because it means Morgan will be more comfortable sleeping on them than she would have been if we'd merely laid down blankets or furs like our ancestors have done in the past.

Minutes later, Emmerich comes out, carrying an armload of bedding, followed by a still-limping Morgan, who is clutching a tasseled pink pillow to her chest. I take it from her, unable to resist nuzzling her temple a little, just to get a whiff of her scent. She reacts immediately, her hand coming to rest on my chest. She gasps when she touches my naked skin, but before she can move away, I put my hand over hers and close my wings around us.

"I told you, you can touch me anytime," I rumble, leaning down to bring my forehead to hers. "I love your hands on me, Morgan."

She moves a step closer, puts her nose right up to my sternum, and draws in a shaky inhale. "You smell so good."

A rumbling purr starts in my chest. She is drawn to me as much as I am to her, but she's human, so she hasn't been taught what to expect, how to recognize her true mates.

"That's your instinct telling you I'm yours." I push back her hair, then dig my fingers into her golden curls and cup the back of her neck to tilt her face up. "If you were a gargoyle, you'd know it on first sight. But we're here to show you. We'll show you everything."

Morgan stares up at me for a long moment, her eyes wide, her pink lips parted, then surges up and kisses me. A bolt of lust slams into me, my entire body going rigid as stone, and my cock thickens in my pants, ready to sink into her soft body. She's more decisive this time, my Morgan, and leads the kiss, stroking her tongue against mine in bold, sensuous strokes. She brings both hands to my shoulders and pulls herself up until her body is flush with mine, her warm curves pressed to my hard chest.

I pick her up without thinking, my hands going to her lush ass to support her weight. She's taller than the usual human woman, and I'm relieved—I can take big handfuls of her and not worry that I might crush her with my strength, that I might hurt her without meaning to.

"Klaus," she breathes when I trail a line of kisses from her mouth to her jaw and down her neck, searching for the spots that make her shiver. "Kiss me."

I obey immediately, fusing my lips to hers again, then suck on her tongue, imagining how she will taste all over. Will she like it when I spread her legs and swipe my tongue over her slick pussy? Because I know it'll be wet for me, I can smell it now, the honeyed notes of her arousal blooming in the air around us.

A door slams, jerking me back to awareness. I was so lost

in Morgan, swept away by lust, that I forgot about Emmerich standing right beside us all this time.

But he's not here anymore.

Slowly, I let Morgan down, hissing as her body slides past my front, teasing my erect cock through my pants. Even that small contact is enough for my control to waver, and my hips jerk forward before I can stop them.

Morgan looks down between us, and her breath escapes on a rush. "Oh, wow. Um. That's…that's impressive."

I try not to preen at her words, but they are exactly what a gargoyle likes to hear. I want to show her every ounce of pleasure, right here, right now, but I shake my head, clearing away the lustful thoughts.

It seems like Morgan hasn't yet noticed that Emmerich has left the room. She must have lost herself to the kiss just as much as I had.

I lower my wings and tuck them close, then take a step back from her and finally release her, even though the pounding need in my chest is telling me I'm a fool. But Emmerich has left, and I need to find out what's going on.

"Where's Emmerich?" Morgan peers into the closet. "He was just here."

Yes, and then I kissed you—for the second time.

Was he jealous of Morgan? Or of me? Whatever it was, I had to make it right.

"He's on the roof." I strain my ears to hear his footsteps. "I'll go talk to him."

Morgan catches me by my wrist before I can so much as take a step. "Wait. Do you think… Should I be the one to go after him?"

I watch her for a long moment, studying her earnest expression, her wide eyes.

"What will you say to him?" I ask.

Emmerich was my mate first, and I know him better than

anyone. This—adding a new mate to the roost—was always going to be a difficult time, a reshifting of our dynamic, but Morgan might not understand this. She might make a blunder we, as a roost, won't easily recover from.

"Do you trust me?" She takes a blanket from the pile Emmerich brought from the closet and drapes it around her shoulders like a cloak. "I want to learn about you. As gargoyles and as men. And I can't do that if you're the one solving my problems for me."

"I do," I tell her. "But this isn't your problem."

"The hell it isn't," she protests, her eyebrows snapping down. "I barged in here on Christmas Eve and wedged myself between you two. I need Emmerich to know that this wasn't my intention, and if he doesn't want me kissing you, he has the right to tell me so. You looming there might make things harder for him. If I fail, though, you can take your turn."

I straighten my shoulders, a small smile tugging up the corner of my mouth despite the fraught situation. Our new mate seemed so timid at first, but that must have been the initial shock of finding out we exist, as well as her injury. Now that she's healing, both from her fall and the surprise, she's a lioness, all sharp claws and protective instincts.

"All right," I tell her. "But you *will* allow me to carry you up the stairs. The last thing we want is for you to hurt yourself again."

CHAPTER 9

MORGAN

I let Klaus lift me in his strong arms and carry me to the spiral staircase and up to the roof of the tower. The conical shape of the spire beside us is covered with a thick layer of snow, as is the landing platform we emerge onto. I recognize my issue the moment the first snowflakes drift onto my blanket—I'm still barefoot, my boots drying downstairs by the fire. And even if they were dry, I wouldn't want to risk shoving my injured foot into one because that would *hurt*.

But Emmerich is there, crouched on the edge of the platform like a Gothic statue, resting in the same position they showed me earlier, his fists on the ground, his wings tucked against his back.

"Let me down," I whisper to Klaus.

He frowns at me. "Your feet will freeze. I will hold you while you two talk."

Emmerich twists halfway, glancing at us over his shoulder. He doesn't come any closer, but he will, I know it. I might be playing on his protective instincts, but I need him to stop sulking—or worse, prevent him from flying off into the night and leaving me alone here with Klaus.

If this new relationship is to work, we'll all have to change our ways. Since they're more statue-like than any other creature I've ever seen, this may be difficult for them, but I know we can make it. The last thing I want is to ruin their relationship, so I will do everything in my power to avoid that.

"You have to let me go," I tell Klaus. "Please, I know what I'm doing."

I'm not—not really. But I'm *hoping* that Emmerich's instinct will prevail, and that seeing me in discomfort will override whatever he's currently thinking.

Klaus frowns at me, his thick black eyebrows drawing together. He sniffs at me as if confirming I'm serious, then blows out a long sigh and carefully lowers me to the snowy floor.

I gasp as my feet hit the ice-cold flagstones. This close to the roof entrance, they're covered with a scant inch of snow, but when I step forward, making my slow way toward Emmerich, the drifts reach my ankles, then rise up my calves.

Damn it. If this doesn't work, I might get cold burn after all.

I half twist around to glance at Klaus. "I'll yell if I need help. Can you wait for us downstairs?"

He stares at me for a moment, then dips his chin in a curt nod and disappears down the stairs. I hope this doesn't mean he's gone off to mope, but I'll deal with him later if I have to. One problem—or gargoyle—at a time.

Emmerich hasn't taken his eyes off me since Klaus brought me up to the roof. He moves slightly now, shifting his position so he can keep me in his sights.

"Hey," I call out, hoping my voice will carry over the whistling wind.

The storm is picking up, and once again, I'm incredibly glad Klaus found me in the forest when he did.

"Go back inside, Morgan," Emmerich replies, his deep voice floating over to me. "It is not safe for you out here."

I stop and cross my arms over my chest to hide my shivering. "I'm not going anywhere unless you come with me."

His frown is visible even through the flurries of snow. "That's not funny. You will die out here. Go down to Klaus, he will keep you warm."

Ah, there we go.

"I want *both* of you there." I shuffle my feet in an effort to keep some feeling in them. "And Klaus needs you, too."

He heaves a deep sigh, then unfurls to his full height, straightening his shoulders. His wings flare out as he shakes the snow from them, and then he's in front of me, moving faster than I would have thought. He's so *big*, so unearthly in this moment, but I'm not afraid. Whether it's this mating thing playing with my emotions or something else, I don't care—all I know is that I feel a deep sense of safety whenever Emmerich and Klaus are near me. It should have been impossible for me to be this relaxed, but I am—with the exception of my freezing feet.

Emmerich swoops down and lifts me into his arms as if he's reading my thoughts. "You're putting yourself at risk. For me. I don't like that."

I shuffle around in his embrace, holding on to the blanket with one hand until I end up with my legs around his waist and my other hand clutching at his shoulder. It's a precarious position, but I know Emmerich won't let me fall.

"What happened?" I ask him softly. "Why did you leave?"

He gazes down at me with his serious blue eyes. The light coming from the staircase is the only illumination up here, and it casts half his face in shadow, reminding me of how handsome he is.

"I was jealous," he admits.

I press my lips together. This is exactly what I didn't want. But we have to clear away this issue, or we'll never work. I want…*more* from them, but I can't possibly take another step with either of them if we're not all on the same page here.

"Of Klaus?" I ask. "Or of me?"

Maybe the first step to healing this rift is figuring out Emmerich's emotions. Or maybe it's removing me from the equation. I might have to ask Klaus to fly me back home after all.

"Both," Emmerich grumbles. "It's a complicated thing, is it not? I want you more than anything, and seeing you in Klaus' arms made me want to rip his wings off. But at the same time, Klaus has been *mine* for so long, I don't know how to share him yet."

He leans his forehead against mine, his skin warm. His exhale steams in the frigid air between us, reminding me that I'll have to return inside soon or risk hypothermia. But I can't leave or ask him to take me downstairs before we figure this out.

"Do you think this is just growing pains?" I ask, my heart constricting as my question formulates in my mind. "Or do you think it'll be impossible for us to stay together as a roost and not end up resenting each other?"

Emmerich blinks, his eyebrows climbing high. "What? I don't think that. I left you alone because *I'm* the problem. I need to get my head on straight and stop fussing, and I didn't want to spoil your evening. We were just starting to build a nest, and you and Klaus looked so cozy together, so—"

I put a hand over his mouth to stop the flood of his

words. "Wait. You *removed* yourself because you thought you would—what? Kill our mood?"

He shrugs as if this isn't a big issue.

"Emmerich!" I smack his hard chest lightly, the gesture awkward from my position. "Your feelings are *important*! You're not supposed to leave whenever you feel a negative emotion."

He frowns and grips me tighter, his hands squeezing my thigh and waist. "But… It was so easy with Klaus."

"You mean before I arrived?" I stare up at him, trying to understand. "You've never fought?"

He scoffs. "Of course we've fought. Have you met him? He would argue about whether the sky is blue on a grumpy day."

"Okay?" I peer into his eyes, still confused. "So what—?"

"I didn't have to share his attention." His wings flare wider as a gust of wind blasts the tower, and he wraps us in a safe cocoon, moving closer to the wall. "And he didn't have to share mine. How can I make sure that neither one of you feels left behind when I am with the other? I want to lavish you with all my love and spend weeks trying to figure out how to make you scream, Morgan, but what will Klaus think of that? And what if he wants to do the same? Will we have to draw up a schedule to make sure no one is abandoned?"

Oh.

"I thought we might…do it all together," I blurt, heat rising in my cheeks. "I mean, I don't… I just didn't even…"

My words fail me as a deep rumble starts in Emmerich's chest. It's a growl and a purr combined, and it vibrates against me, more sensation than sound.

"Together?" he demands. "You—you would do that?"

I open my mouth to reply, but he's already moving. He throws the door to the stairway wide and stomps down the stairs, barely pausing to latch the door behind us. He holds me tight to his chest and moves one hand to the back of my neck to press me closer, as if he's worried he might drop me.

"Klaus!" he calls the moment he bursts into their main living room. "Did you know Morgan wants us *both* to be with her? At the same time?"

"Oh my God," I groan, thumping my forehead against his chest. "Emmerich! What did we say about—"

"I thought it had to be one or the other, with someone always being left out," my gargoyle continues, his deep voice rising in excitement. "But if we can be together, all three of us, no one will be sad."

A beat of silence follows his declaration, and I finally force myself to lift my head and look at Klaus. He's kneeling in the nest, stuffing a pillow into a deep-purple pillowcase, the tassels on the corners twitching merrily with his every movement. But he stills now, then slowly lowers the cushion to his lap.

"Is that what you were worried about?" he asks, his deep voice low. "That Morgan and I would abandon you?"

"Yes," Emmerich admits. "Or that you would feel alone when I'm with her, or—"

"Or that I would be hurt, yes," I finish for him. "And that might still happen. We won't *always* be able to be together as a trio."

"But most of the time?" Emmerich asks, focusing back on me.

I flush under his intense scrutiny. "I think we can agree to do that, yeah. Most of the time."

We both turn to look at Klaus, who is staring at us as if we're mad.

"What?" I ask.

He shakes his head. "I've heard of roosts like that. But I didn't think… Not with…"

"Not with me," I finish, a lump forming in my throat. "Is that it?"

He pushes himself to his feet and comes closer. I squirm in Emmerich's arms until he puts me down, and I take a step away from him, even though my body is telling me this is a terrible idea. I should be trying to get *closer* to the amazingly gorgeous gargoyle, not moving in the opposite direction.

But I need to stand on my own two feet for this conversation, even if my ankle still hurts a bit. I grit my teeth and do my best not to show it, but Klaus frowns at me and nudges me backward until I take one of the chairs they brought closer to the fire earlier.

Then he crouches in front of me so I don't have to crane my neck, and my heart does a stupid little flip because he's always thinking of me, trying to make me as comfortable as possible.

I've never had that with anyone. I didn't even feel this respected with Andy, and I was set to marry him.

I don't know what that says about me or my choice in men. Honestly, I don't think I should be drawing any conclusions or making decisions right now. It's been such a long day, and if I wasn't so certain we need to finish this conversation, I'd ask the guys to just let me go to bed.

But Klaus' gray eyes are serious, and he clearly has something to say, so I swallow down the hurt and uncertainty and nod for him to continue.

"You are human," he says slowly, as if choosing his words with care. "And we're not."

I squint at him, trying to see where he's getting at. "Yes, I know," I say finally. "Is that an issue?"

Emmerich joins us, settling in the armchair I rested in earlier. He reaches out and takes my hand, then rubs my palm with his thumbs, as if softening me up for whatever is coming, but I like it too much to pull my hand away from him.

Klaus shakes his head, his silky black hair slipping over his shoulders. He has silvery strands in it, starting at his temples, and somehow that makes him even more attractive to me.

"When gargoyles fuck, we like to…" He pauses and glances at Emmerich, then groans and rattles off a few words in German.

Before I can get worried about what he's saying, Emmerich grins at him, then focuses on me.

"We like to fuck a lot. And loudly. And hard," he explains, pressing harder on my palm.

I bite back a groan of pleasure, my eyelids fluttering. "I don't see a problem with that."

Klaus drags a palm down his face. "Do you know how gargoyles were created?"

I blink at the sudden change in conversation. "Uh, no? Evolution, I assume?"

His lips twitch up in the corners, just slightly, a hint of a smile. "Legend says we were born out of stone. Supposedly, our ancestors were statues, guarding buildings and protecting their inhabitants, but one day, a particularly powerful witch decided she needed more than just a scary statue on her roof and breathed life into her sculptures."

"Oh." I squirm, my analytical mind churning. "But, um, that's probably just a story, right? I don't know what evolutionary branch you're from just yet, but I bet your ancestors crawled out of the primordial soup, just like mine did."

Now they're staring at me like I've gone mad, so I wave a hand to indicate it doesn't matter.

"Okay, let's say your origin story is true," I say quickly. "What of it?"

"We are made of stone," Klaus says, "or something like it.

You, on the other hand, are not, and if we fucked you like we want—and worse, if we did it together—we could hurt you. Irreparably."

Emmerich is nodding along, his handsome face creased in worry. "Yes, he is right. You could get injured."

Heat floods my body at their words. My inner guidance system must clearly be broken because I shouldn't—under any circumstance—be turned on by this, but Emmerich is sitting right *there*, telling me he's hard for me, and my brain can't deal with this anymore.

"Okay." I blow out a long breath, trying to get myself under control before they figure out which way my mind has gone. "Are you saying you'll never be able to fuck me *properly*, like you want, because I'm too soft for you?"

"No," Klaus says.

At the same time, Emmerich nods and affirms, "Yes."

They exchange worried glances, then focus back on me.

"We don't know," Klaus says. "Neither of us has ever been with a human before, so we will need to figure it out."

Emmerich purses his lips, then adds, "There is no doubt. You are our roost mate, and I don't want anyone else but you. So there must be a way, or the Fates wouldn't have paired us together."

I stare at him, doubt gnawing at me. "What if there's been...some sort of cosmic glitch?" I motion from myself to them and back. "I mean, this doesn't exactly bode well. How do you know we're *right*?"

Emmerich frowns, then moves, reaching for me so fast, I can barely let out a squeak before I'm in his lap, his warm body surrounding me. He takes my chin gently and leans in to press his mouth to mine. It starts as a tame kiss, just a brush of our lips and a hint of tongue, but the moment his fresh scent fills my nose, my restraint evaporates. I put my palms on his chest and run them up to his shoulders, marveling at the warm, leathery texture of his skin. I angle my head to the side to deepen our kiss, and Emmerich lets me, a groan starting in his throat. I drink up the sound and lick his lower lip, then shiver as he trails nibbling kisses over my jaw, to the point below my ear.

His big hands come to my waist, and he squeezes me, then moves me closer to him, so his hardness nudges my thigh. It's impressive, but despite all their warnings, I want to know what it would feel like. If he's right, if *this* is really what's written in the stars for us, I want it all.

"Morgan," he groans.

I press myself to his chest and shift my hips, rolling them as my pussy clenches around emptiness, so needy and desperate for him, I'm seconds away from tearing open the front of his leather trousers and taking him in my hand.

Then he tightens his hold on my hips and moves me back to my chair. The loss of his heat and touch is immediate, and I let out an embarrassing whine, reaching forward to keep a hold on him.

Emmerich lets out a low chuckle and entwines his fingers with mine, squeezing lightly. "There was no glitch. I've never felt need so strong before, apart from with Klaus. Have you?"

His serious gray-blue gaze bores into me, daring me to lie.

"Never," I tell him earnestly. "So…what now?"

Klaus, who has been watching us with feral intensity, finally lets loose a long breath. "Now, we go to bed. You are tired and injured, and there's no rush. You have the holidays off work, yes?"

"Yes. I have more than a week. Are you suggesting I spend it all with you?" I raise one eyebrow at him. "That's moving fast, at least in human terms."

But he doesn't rise to the challenge. Instead, a wicked grin stretches his lips, and he shows me his sharp fangs. "We're not human, *Engel*. You'd do well to remember that."

CHAPTER 10

EMMERICH

I carry Morgan downstairs for a quick trip to the bathroom, then bring her over to our nest. She fits so well in my arms, I don't want to let go, but I don't want to scare her, so I deposit her gently on the edge of the mattresses that Klaus had tied together and stand to let her settle in.

Morgan's hand shoots out before I can move away, and she grabs my wrist, holding on to it tightly. "Are you leaving?"

She gazes up at me, her brown eyes wide, her expression crestfallen. I can't help it—I crouch in front of her, take her chin between two fingers, and press a crushing kiss to her lips. She tastes like the toothpaste she borrowed from Klaus, but underneath it, her essence comes through, the honeyed notes driving my need higher.

"I'm not going anywhere if you want me close," I tell her. "You only have to say it."

She nibbles on her lower lip, then gives my hand a little tug. "I want you to stay."

Pride flares inside me, hot and potent. My mate wants *me*. It makes me want to beat my chest and pin her to me, strip off the soft layers of her clothing and find her slick heat.

Then I remember Klaus—and our promise that we would try to do this *together*.

I glance over my shoulder to find him watching us from the kitchen, where he's been washing the same cup for several minutes. His hands are sudsy and his grip so strong, it's a wonder he hasn't crushed the cup. With a quick twitch of my head, I indicate the nest, then shrug as if to ask whether he's coming to bed.

He hesitates a moment, his expression stormy. Then he gives me a small nod and rinses the cup, then dries his hands on a kitchen towel, his movements deliberate. Is he giving us time to settle? Or waiting for me to change my mind and demand the right to spend the first night with Morgan alone?

I shuffle as far to the left as I comfortably can and tug Morgan down next to me, leaving the right side of the nest empty. I hope that's enough of a message for him—there is space for all of us here.

Then I lie flat on my back, careful not to hit Morgan with my wing, and undo the button on my leather pants.

"What are you doing?" Morgan asks suddenly, her voice higher than before.

I glance up to find her staring at me. "It's hot in here. I will be uncomfortable under the blankets if I don't remove these."

Her cheeks have turned a deep shade of pink, and her eyes are slightly glassy and unfocused. "You sleep naked?"

"How else should I be sleeping?" I frown at her, confused.

I can't imagine wearing leather pants all night if I don't need to. "Is this a human thing?"

She lets out a strangled laugh. "Yeah, I guess it is. With—with people we've only just met, we rarely get fully naked together unless we mean to fuck."

My eyebrows climb up. "What?" I turn to Klaus. "Are you hearing this?"

He chuckles, the sound low and wicked. "We did warn her. We are not human."

Morgan looks from me to him and back. "Yeah. You said that." She pushes back her hair and grabs on to it for a moment, clearly thinking things through. "Okay. How about this—you can get naked whenever you want. I'd hate to cramp your style."

There's a naughty glint in her eyes as she says it, and I can't help but laugh.

"That's very kind," I tease her. "And what of you? Gargoyles run hotter than humans. You'll be sleeping between us tonight. It would be such a pity if you were uncomfortably warm."

She releases her hair, some of the tension melting from her. "I'll sleep in my underwear and t-shirt. That means I'm only interested in *sleeping* tonight, okay?"

I nod, catching on to her plan. "And when you remove all your clothes, you'll be interested in fucking."

"Exactly," Morgan says, sounding very pleased with herself.

Behind her, Klaus shoves down his pants, freeing his cock. It's hard for her—for us—and leaking at the tip, but he presses his palm down on it, then lowers himself quickly and draws a blanket over his lap. I want to do the same, unwilling to scare Morgan with the size of my fully grown dick, but she's facing me, her lips parted slightly, the vein in her neck pulsing faster than before.

Is she waiting for me to undress?

Wicked little human.

I won't leave her dissatisfied, though. By now, I think I'm wholly incapable of refusing any of her wishes, which might become a problem sometime in the future, but right now, our interests align. She wants to see my cock, and I want to show it to her, even if there's no touching on the horizon for tonight.

I undo the last of the buttons, lift my hips, and shove down my pants. Quicker than ever, I kick them off my feet and dump them over the edge of the nest, then stretch on my back, canting my body slightly in Morgan's direction.

Her shocked gasp is music to my ears. My cock is as long as Klaus', or nearly, but slightly thicker. Morgan will be very pleased once I work it inside her. It will fill her pussy completely, and she must know it, too, because she's turning a deeper shade of red.

"Oh my God," she whispers, her hand coming to cover her mouth.

"It's hard for you." I grasp the root loosely to show off the shaft. I don't squeeze too hard, because it wouldn't take long for me to come, and I don't want to embarrass myself. "Do you like it?"

She swallows thickly and lowers her hand. "I mean…yes? It's—it's a very nice cock, Emmerich. But have you ever seen a human dick? They're, ah, they're smaller. In general. This is…a lot."

I sniff the air between us, and my heart skips a beat. She's *nervous*, and there's a hint of something else—is it fear? Or worse, disgust?

My disappointment is swift and utterly devastating. I grab the nearest blanket and yank it over my lap to hide the cock that is clearly upsetting her. From behind her, Klaus is staring at me, his expression inscrutable. He's not angry—but he isn't happy about this development either.

"I'm sorry." Morgan sits back on her heels. "I didn't mean to hurt your feelings."

"You didn't," I say gruffly. It's a lie, but the last thing I want is to shove my cock at her when she clearly doesn't want it. "Let's just go to sleep."

Her eyebrows draw together in a frown. "No, Emmerich. Remember what we said about talking through the things that bother us?"

I glower up at her, feeling petulant and embarrassed at the same time. It's not a pleasant combination, and I want nothing more than to roll away from her, pull my pants back on, and stomp away.

But that would hurt *Morgan's* feelings, and that's not something I can do.

"It's okay if you don't like it," I say slowly. "But I wanted to show you."

She nods, her expression gentling. "It's—it's very big. That's why I freaked out. You really haven't seen a human cock before?"

Klaus clears his throat. "Like you said, humans rarely get naked in public. We haven't had the opportunity."

Morgan opens her mouth as if she wants to say something, then shakes her head. "You know what? Never mind human cocks. Let's just say they're smaller than yours and don't have those, ah, ridges. They look interesting, by the way."

She's talking fast, still flustered, but her scent isn't as nervous anymore, and she doesn't smell upset either.

"So you've never been fucked with a cock this size?" I grin at her, relishing the news.

The color of her cheeks deepens. "No."

"But you're willing to try?" Klaus leans close to her.

"Yeah," she breathes. "I'd like that. Very much."

He takes her hand and kisses the inside of her palm, then presses it against his cheek, as if being held by her is all he's ever wanted.

I understand the sentiment perfectly.

Shuffling closer, I put my hands on Morgan's waist and tug her down so she's lying between us, safe in our nest. She squeaks, then removes her glasses and sets them aside, blinking a little as if to refocus her gaze. The scent of her arousal blooms in the air, and I groan, then lean in for a kiss. I lick into her mouth to taste her incredible essence.

Klaus rumbles approvingly and settles on her other side, his wing open over us both, always the protector. "We should let Morgan rest, Emmerich."

I lift my head, dazed from Morgan's kisses. He's right, of course, but Morgan doesn't seem to agree—she's got her fingers in my hair and tugs on the back of my head to bring my lips back to hers.

And who am I to refuse my mate?

I kiss her again, my hand on her hip, so close to where I want to go but still so far. Tentatively, I slip my fingers to the hem of her t-shirt and push it up just an inch, enough to feel her soft, warm skin.

A groan rips itself from my throat, and I wrench myself back before my instincts take over and I demand more from her than she's willing to give. Putting some distance between us, I stare at her, chest heaving with quick, shallow breaths.

"Sorry." Morgan presses her fingers to her swollen lips. Then she grins up at me. "You're a great kisser. I enjoyed that a lot."

My purr fills the room, a deep sound that I've only ever uttered when Klaus has just fucked me well. My cock twitches at the thought of it, and I glance at him to find him watching me with a hungry gaze, his nostrils flaring.

He must be scenting my need—but I wonder if he knows it's for him as much as Morgan.

He rears up and moves in suddenly, but instead of kissing Morgan, like I expected him to, he palms the back of my neck and draws me in for a rough, possessive kiss. His tongue thrusts in my mouth, demanding submission, and I give it willingly, clutching on to his shoulder.

The kiss is a reminder of what we are together—of what we *were* and always will be, even though our roost now has a new member. I want him to know I feel the same, that I'll always want him, so I kiss him back, giving him all of me.

When he pulls back, he stares at me for a moment, his serious expression so solemn, I know he understood what I tried to tell him. Then he glances down at Morgan, and the corners of his lips turn up.

I follow his gaze to find our human mate with her lips parted, her eyes round as saucers. She's lying very still, as if afraid to draw attention to herself, but she didn't miss a moment of our kiss.

"Are you all right?" Klaus asks.

She nods mutely, her throat working as she swallows. I lean down to sniff her neck and grin, satisfied.

"She's more than all right," I tell Klaus. "She smells delicious. She liked this as much as we did."

Morgan slaps my shoulder lightly. "What did we say about sniffing people?"

But there's no real anger in her eyes, nor does she move away from me. On the contrary—when I lie next to her, she shuffles closer until our legs are touching and her warm breath ghosts over my arm.

Klaus takes her other side and studies her, running his gaze over her luscious form. "You're still clothed."

Morgan squirms at the reminder. "I know."

I put my palm on her soft belly, keeping the pressure light. "Do you want help? I am very good at disrobing."

She groans. "Of course you are."

I slip my little finger to the sliver of skin visible above the waistband of her leggings. She jerks under my touch but doesn't push my hand away—instead, her eyelids flutter, and she takes a shuddering breath.

"Morgan?" Klaus prompts. "Do you want help?"

For a moment, the question hangs between us. Then she gives us a minute nod—and it's all the permission we need.

I pinch the waistband of her leggings and tug it down. Morgan helps by lifting her hips, and I draw the stretchy, patterned fabric over her lush hips, exposing black cotton underwear—and a *lot* of skin. I stare at her creamy thighs, arrested.

Morgan's scent intensifies, the honeyed notes of her arousal growing stronger. She's turned on by my staring. I glance up at her for a second, meeting her heated gaze, then look down at the apex of her thighs again, where her pussy is hidden by that scrap of fabric, so, so close.

A growl tears itself from my throat. It's a low sound, and it reverberates around the room, its intensity building.

"Emmerich," Klaus barks, a clear warning.

But I'm too far gone. This is our *mate* and she needs me, her body calling out to me. I know we said we'd only be sleeping tonight, but even as I try to calm myself, each inhale brings more of her scent into my lungs, the call of her too strong to resist.

Klaus told Morgan we weren't human, but she doesn't know what this means, not really.

It's not about the wings or the horns, or even the dick she was so afraid of.

It's the instinct that's telling me to rut, to mate her and

breed her until she's pregnant with my young. It's the insatiable need that overshadows all civilized rules, tearing past everything I've learned about human society because the beast inside me doesn't care.

It only wants *her*.

CHAPTER 11

MORGAN

Emmerich's growl is a living thing, a sound so deep it vibrates through my body, disrupting my peace and tickling my instincts. My breaths quicken at the realization that I'm the one responsible—it must be my body's reaction to him that's causing this in him.

One part of my mind is desperately curious about the process. I want to study the phenomenon, to learn how quickly my scent could drive him to this feral state. Another part of me is afraid, and I think it's the most logical—I'm being undressed by a mythological monster, and he's staring down at me as if he wants to devour me.

But the third slice of my mind is screaming "Yes!" so loudly, it drowns out all the rest. It's why I lower my hands to my belly and pull up my t-shirt just a little, showing Emmerich an inch of skin, exposing my belly button. It's why I widen my thighs, a daring, possibly deranged move when he's barely holding back.

Klaus puts a hand over mine, stopping me from lifting my t-shirt any higher. "Are you sure?" he asks, his voice gravelly.

I glance from Emmerich to him. His dark eyebrows are drawn together, his fangs bared, and I realize he's not much better off—he merely has a better grip on his impulses than his roost mate. Klaus' chest heaves with every breath, his nostrils flaring wide as he inhales more of me, looming over my body.

It's a loaded question. Am I sure I want…whatever Emmerich wants to do with me? How can I be, when I don't even know what he intends to do? Am I absolutely certain I trust them enough to believe that they'll stop if I ask them to?

I shouldn't be.

But whatever force is working its magic on them, tying them so closely to me, it's got me in its grip as well.

"Yeah," I whisper. "I'm sure. But—no cocks tonight."

The corner of Klaus' mouth tips up, and his intense glare softens for just a moment. "All right. No cocks."

"I-I want to," I say quickly. "But we'll have to go slow, and I don't think Emmerich can go slow right now."

Emmerich's gaze snaps up to me, and he opens his mouth as if to protest, but I reach up and palm his cheek, and he leans into my touch like a giant cat, closing his eyes and rumbling some more.

"It's okay," I murmur. "I understand. And I want…whatever it is you need to do."

His chest expands on a deep breath, then he closes his eyes and drops his chin as if my permission was the release he was waiting for. His wings flare wide, then come over Klaus and me like a canopy, creating a cocoon of safety. He kneels at my feet and yanks my leggings off in one swift movement, then settles between my open thighs.

"Easy," Klaus warns when Emmerich grasps my knees and shoves them wider. "Take off her panties first."

Emmerich glowers at him, and by the way he hooks his fingers in the elastic waistband of my panties, I know he's thinking of ripping them.

"They're my only pair." I lift my hips to help him get them off. "I'll need them for tomorrow."

He draws them down slowly, his warm hands skimming my skin. "You won't need them tomorrow. We'll spend all day in the nest."

They're the first words he's uttered since he snapped into this wild mood, and I can't help but laugh.

"Good plan," I tell him. "But I don't—ah!"

My hips jerk up at the first contact of his fingers with my pussy. I'm not wet enough yet for him to push inside me, but he doesn't rush me—he puts two fingertips to the hood of my clit and spreads me, staring right down at me.

"You're all pink and slick." He tilts his head, his expression curious. "Klaus, did you know humans were like this?"

I let out a breathless laugh. "Uh, yeah. That's—that's what human pussies are like, for the most part." I shiver as he moves his fingers slightly, spreading my lips to peer at the opening of my pussy. "Well, the color varies, I guess, and some women shave, but I haven't…"

I'm babbling, nervous and uncertain of what he'll do next. Lifting myself up on my elbows, I study him. He holds himself perfectly still, his focus complete. I glance at Klaus, but he's staring, too, leaning in as if he doesn't want to miss a second of this show.

Gods, this would be so embarrassing if it wasn't *them*. But they said they've never been with a human, so I can't really be mad about any of this. Maybe they're simply unsure of what to do with me?

"Do you need me to tell you what to do?" I ask, breaking the silence. "How to make me feel good, I mean."

At that, Emmerich glances up again. "I want to lick you. You smell delicious. Will that feel good?"

My breath rushes out. "Yeah. If you'd like. That'll feel really good."

He settles between my spread thighs, and in a smooth move, dips his hands under my ass and lifts me to his mouth. I lose my balance and topple back onto the pillows with a surprised huff, but before I can do so much as push my hair away from my face, Emmerich puts his mouth to my pussy and drags his long tongue over me from my taint to my clit.

The rough surface of his tongue feels *amazing*. It's hot—hotter than my sensitive flesh—and unlike anything I've experienced so far. My lips part on a surprised exhale as he dips between my pussy lips and spears his tongue inside me, the pointed tip flicking just shy of my G-spot.

"Oh my…" I reach between my legs and grab a handful of his thick hair. "W-what…? Oh God, this feels so good."

Klaus' chuckle pulls me from my shocked stupor, and I look up to find him staring at my face, studying my reactions. He cups my cheek with one large hand and runs the pad of his thumb over my lower lip.

"Your face is so expressive," he murmurs. "Every emotion shown so clearly. I don't even need to smell you to know you're enjoying this."

I suck the tip of his thumb in my mouth and flick my tongue over it. It's a teasing, erotic move, one I never thought I'd make, but Klaus seems to love it. His gray eyes flash with heat, and he presses down on my tongue, then reaches deeper.

"Is this what you like, Morgan?" He moves closer, his grip on my chin tightening. "I can't wait to show you everything we can do together."

My eyelids flutter shut as Emmerich circles my clit with the tip of his tongue, and I can't hold back a moan. He interprets the sound correctly and focuses on the spot, alternating teasing flicks with long lashes of his rough tongue. The pleasure builds inside me, slow and insistent, just as I like.

Then something touches my leg, a warm, narrow band looping around my thigh. I open my eyes to find Emmerich's tail winding around my leg. Gods—it feels like he's trying to get closer to me in any way possible, so I give him what he wants, hooking my legs over his shoulders and digging my heels into his back.

Emmerich groans when my calves rub his wings, so I do it again, repeating the movement until he's thrusting wildly against the bed, his hips working, his breaths coming faster, hot on my wet flesh.

"You look so good together." Klaus runs his fingers through Emmerich's hair. "I never thought I'd enjoy *watching* so much."

I cry out at his words, because holy hell, how does he know exactly what I need to hear?

"Emmerich is so close to coming, *Engel*," he purrs in my ear. "He loves it when you pull his hair. He loves having his wings rubbed even more."

The gargoyle between my legs whimpers, and I know Klaus is right. I brush his hand away and take over, tugging on Emmerich's hair lightly to keep him right where I need him.

"What do you need?" Klaus asks, his hand on my belly now. "Can you come just from Emmerich licking your pussy?"

"M-maybe," I stutter, clutching on to his arm with my other hand. "Kiss me?"

He swoops down to press his lips to mine, and I lose myself in his kiss, each lick and suck so perfectly in tune with

Emmerich's. They coax my pleasure higher, and when Klaus nips my lower lip with his sharp teeth, I cry out, my body trembling on the edge of release.

"Stop me if I go too far," Klaus murmurs against my lips.

The next moment, his hand slips under my t-shirt. He reaches my bra and tugs it up in one swift move, then wraps his big hand around my breast, squeezing. His clawed fingers prick my skin, but not enough to hurt—and he stares down at me intently, gauging my reactions. When he pinches my nipple between two fingers, hard, I flop back on the bed, moaning.

"There we go," he says, his grin turning wicked. "I knew you'd like that. I'll learn every single thing that makes you sing so prettily for us. We'll stay in this nest until you're limp with pleasure and you can't take even a drop more of our cum."

My belly tightens at his words, and I whimper, my thighs shaking. "Oh, fuck, yes! That. I want that."

Klaus' chuckle is low and wicked, and he switches sides, palming my other breast, exploring me. Then he glances down at Emmerich and says, "Slip the tip of your tail into her pussy and suck on her clit."

It takes my hazy brain a moment to comprehend the words. It's when I feel a slick, warm pressure at my pussy lips that I realize it's not Emmerich's tongue but his tail, the length of it still wrapped around my leg.

"What?"

I try to lift myself on my elbows to see what he's doing, but Klaus flattens his palm on my chest, not shoving down, just holding me lightly in place.

"Trust us?" he murmurs.

All the tension goes out from me because I do—otherwise, I wouldn't be lying here, spread open and mostly naked, trembling on the verge of my climax.

"Good," he purrs when I stretch out beside him. "You're being so good for us, Morgan. Now let him in. He'll make you come so hard."

Emmerich's groan reverberates around the room. He's close, too, and the knowledge that he's enjoying this so much, he'll likely come without even touching his cock, is enough for me to relax completely. I grip his hair tighter to show him I like this, then spread my legs a little more, making room for him.

The tip of his tail circles the opening of my pussy, the sensation similar to that of a finger, only thicker, and when he spreads my lower lips and pushes inside, I can't hold back the gasp of pleasure.

"That feels *amazing*," I choke out. "Emmerich!"

He lets out a huffing laugh and presses a quick kiss to my inner thigh. "And you taste like heaven, *Liebchen*."

He fuses his lips to my clit, and I nearly levitate off the bed. I'm so sensitive already, the pleasure is almost too much, but I need *more*, I need them to show me everything, just like Klaus promised.

"Hook the tip up," I gasp. "There's a-a spot I like... *Oh, fuck yes!*"

Emmerich follows my instructions to the letter, and when the tip of his tail brushes my G-spot, my mind blanks out. Klaus gives me a feral grin, then pinches my nipple hard, and my orgasm rolls over me in a tidal wave of pleasure.

Klaus spits out a string of German words, then crushes his mouth to mine, drinking up my cries, his hands on me possessive and sure. Emmerich draws out my climax with slow licks of his tongue over my clit, sending aftershocks through my nerves, until I'm a trembling, sobbing mess.

Then he pulls his tail out and swoops down to clean my slick pussy, and that's what tips him over—his guttural groan is half muffled by my flesh, but his hips buck against the bed, and his big body shudders between my legs. I reach down and smooth my palm over his wing, and it flares wider as he twitches and moans.

"Incredible," Klaus whispers. "You two are so good together. Look at how hard you made him come, Morgan."

A glow of pride fills my chest, and I can't help but smile at Emmerich, who lifts his head, his eyes hazy with pleasure.

"That was amazing," I tell him.

He drops down for another lick, and I shiver, then tug on his horns to get him to join me. He glances down at himself, then swipes his cum away with the already sticky sheet and tosses it over the edge of the nest.

I guess that's one of the reasons why they piled so many blankets, pillows, and sheets on here—things are bound to get messy.

Emmerich crawls up and lowers himself beside me with a huff. "I enjoyed this a lot."

His words are so serious, so solemn, I can't help but giggle.

"Yeah," I murmur. "I did, too."

We both glance at Klaus, who's been watching us all this time, his big body taut with tension. My mouth dries up at the sight of his expression—he looks like he wants to devour us both. I want to ask if he wants to come, too, especially since the sheet covering his lap isn't doing much to disguise his big erection, but before I can suggest something, he leans over me and kisses Emmerich full on the mouth.

It's a deep, rough kiss, and Emmerich *melts* for him, shoving his hand in Klaus' long hair, moaning.

"You taste like her," Klaus rasps. "So fucking amazing."

After a moment, he draws back and lies next to me, his wings folded, his gaze fixed on the ceiling.

"Klaus?" I ask tentatively. "Are you okay?"

He slants his gaze at me, his eyes dark in the light of the dying fire. "Yes."

Huh.

I purse my lips, not knowing how to get through to him. Then Emmerich wraps his arm around me from behind, pulling me into the warmth of his body.

"Go to sleep, *Liebchen*," he murmurs.

"But—" I squirm, trying to sit up, even though he feels so cozy and warm. "Emmerich, let go. Klaus—tell him to release me."

Klaus turns on his side, facing us. "It's all right, Morgan. I am perfectly satisfied tonight."

I stop my struggles to get away from Emmerich. "You are? But you didn't even come."

"No," he agrees. "And that's all right."

I narrow my eyes at him, my curiosity burning bright. He seemed to be really into it earlier, kissing and touching me, and he is definitely still hard. But if he doesn't want this, if he's holding himself back, the last thing I want to do is make him uncomfortable.

"Okay." I give him a considering look. "I don't understand, but I trust you to know what you need."

It's the same consideration they've shown me, so I definitely won't push if he doesn't want me to.

"He bites," Emmerich murmurs sleepily. His arm has grown heavy at my waist, as if he's already slipping into dreamland.

I half turn to face him. "What?"

"Klaus," he explains, opening one eye. "He likes to bite. It's why he's holding back. If he lost control and you weren't prepared, it would hurt you."

My mind whirrs, processing the new information. Emmerich lets out a low hum and snuggles closer to me, his breath warm on my neck. I'm still wearing my t-shirt and bra, though it's all pushed up and uncomfortable, so I roll around as much as Emmerich will allow me and manage to remove my bra through the sleeve of my t-shirt, all to give myself time to think.

When I settle back on the pillow, I find Klaus watching me, his expression wary. Emmerich's breaths have deepened. The moment seems oddly intimate, Klaus and I still awake while Emmerich sleeps next to us.

"Is that true?" I whisper. "You didn't want to hurt me?"

Klaus reaches out and brushes back my hair. "Yes. It's… instinctual. A possessive claiming. Emmerich enjoys it, so I don't have to hold back with him, but if you were caught by surprise and tensed up instead of relaxing, the bite *would* hurt."

I catch his wrist and bring his palm to my cheek, relishing the warmth. "Why didn't you just tell me?"

He shrugs, though he doesn't pull away. "You were already overwhelmed. We are monsters, after all, and you've only learned of us tonight."

"Yeah, but I didn't have an issue with Emmerich fucking me with his tail, did I?" My cheeks flush with warmth at that, but I'm a *scientist*, goddammit. I won't be embarrassed by talking about sex. "I would rather know than have you protect me by keeping me ignorant."

A corner of his firm lips tips up. "All right. I'll keep that in mind."

I yawn, my tiredness returning now that my body is wrung out and sated. "Is there anything else you need to tell me?"

"Our cum glows in the dark," he says.

I lift my head, my eyes widening. "Wait, really?" I glance to the edge of the nest where Emmerich deposited the messy sheet. "I didn't see anything…"

But Klaus' grin betrays him, telling me he's just messing

with me. I slap his chest lightly, my hand bouncing off his hard muscles.

"You're evil," I grumble. "Making jokes at the naive human's expense."

He chuckles and leans close, brushing a quick kiss across my lips. "Forgive me, I couldn't resist."

Emmerich murmurs something in his sleep, and his wing flares wide, covering my lower body like a leathery blanket. My heart swells with something too vulnerable to name, so I swallow down the emotion and glance back up at Klaus. He's watching me closely, and I know he saw the flicker of what I felt because he kisses me again, more softly this time, lingering and licking. It's the best kiss I've ever experienced, and I return every caress, every touch.

Finally, he draws back, his chest heaving with a deep sigh. "Go to sleep, Morgan."

I love how raspy his voice gets when he's all worked up.

"Will you sleep with us?" I ask, hoping my words don't sound too needy.

The smile he gives me is wicked and tender at the same time.

"Nothing could keep me away from you."

CHAPTER 12

KLAUS

I lied to Morgan when she asked me if I was going to sleep with them. I didn't want to miss a moment of this bliss, so I remained awake all night, watching over my mates as they rested. Emmerich's snores didn't seem to bother Morgan at all, and they curled together, sleeping through the gray light of early dawn.

The wind had picked up during the night, howling around the tower. If Morgan will want to leave today, we might have trouble flying her home safely. But I'm hoping she won't mind staying another day, at least, and give us a chance to show her more of what it means to be a gargoyle's mate.

She stirs now, her eyelids fluttering, so I caress her cheek with my knuckles, lulling her back to sleep. I have to be so careful with her, so gentle, making sure I don't grip her too tightly or move too fast, breaking her delicate bones.

Emmerich spoke the truth when he told her about my impulsive biting issue. It has never been a problem—he loves it when I sink my teeth into his skin, and I've used that to my advantage so many times over the years. If I time it right and bite down on the correct spot on his neck, I can push him over the edge of his climax so easily.

But Morgan is *human*. I could tear her skin with my sharp teeth. I could rend her tendons or even a vein, causing irreparable harm.

Does that mean I won't ever be able to have my mate?

The thought is too painful to contemplate. When I told Morgan we like to fuck hard, I wasn't joking—but my issues go deeper than Emmerich's, so we'll have to be very careful going forward. Last night, I nearly broke, especially when I tasted her essence on Emmerich's lips. Both their scents combined were nearly enough to send me to madness, and if this goes any further, Morgan might not be safe with me, no matter how much I want to protect her.

A low growl starts in my chest at the thought of letting her go, and I breathe in deeply to relax. The last thing Morgan needs is to wake up with a monster growling in her face.

Emmerich is the first to awaken fully. He blinks, his beautiful eyes focusing immediately on the human woman between us. Sometime in the night, she shuffled closer to him, her delectable, naked ass nesting against his groin, but when I tried to move away at about three in the morning to give them more space, she grumbled in her sleep and grabbed the edge of my wing. It was the most endearing, heart-rending gesture, and she wasn't even aware of it.

It told me she feels our presence, too. No matter her human nature, she's affected by this mating bond stretching between us. I can only hope this also means she's strong enough to sustain two gargoyle mates without injury.

She stirs in her sleep, then grumbles and buries her face in the pillows. Emmerich strokes her hip, the move languid, but his expression tells me how he's really feeling—he looks almost reverent, so gentle and hopeful.

"What time is it?" Morgan mumbles, her voice adorably croaky.

I glance over at the clock on the mantelpiece. "Just after nine. Did you sleep well?"

With a huff, she rolls to her back and stretches, her t-shirt riding high and exposing her belly. I fixate on the spot, studying the perfect divot of her belly button, wondering if she'd find it strange if I licked it. Then the temptation becomes too strong, so I lower my head and place the tip of my tongue into the small dip, tasting her skin.

Morgan jerks, then pushes my head away, holding on to my horns to keep me from licking her again. "Stop, stop!"

I twitch away from her in horror. "I'm sorry, Morgan, I'm so sorry. Does it hurt?"

Shame descends on me, swift and bitter. Did she think I was going to bite her? Is she *afraid* of me?

But her scent remains calm—if anything, there's a hint of her sweet arousal, perhaps a remnant from last night or the product of having Emmerich's cock pressed to her ass for most of the night.

She keeps a hold on my horns, making it impossible to shift farther away. She gives me a little yank, and I follow her movement until I'm hovering over her, my hair forming a curtain around my face.

"Hey," she says. "It *tickled*. Your hair tickled my belly when you licked me. I'm not hurt. I liked it, but you surprised me."

"What's tickling?" Emmerich rumbles from behind her.

I've heard the word, and I know what it means—in theory. But I've never experienced it, so it never even occurred to me…

"You're not ticklish?" Morgan scrambles to a seated position and stares down at Emmerich. "Not even a little?"

He shrugs. "Maybe I am but I don't know it?"

Morgan's eyes get that determined glint I'm starting to associate with her scientific brain—she's curious and intends to research this issue.

She reaches out and trails her fingers along Emmerich's ribs, pressing down lightly from time to time. When he doesn't react, she moves on to his belly and tries again, then crawls down to his legs to tease his knees, then finally the soles of his feet. I think she must have forgotten she's only wearing her t-shirt—she's too distracted by this new discovery.

I watch, amusement building inside me. She's *perfect*. Any other human would have run from us, screaming, but we found one who's not only unafraid but genuinely interested in us.

"Nothing?" She glances over her shoulder, her hair mussed and wild.

Emmerich grins at her. "It feels nice to have your hands on me. And my cock is growing very hard for you, especially now that I'm looking at your naked ass."

"Oh!" Morgan's face flushes, and she quickly sits, then gathers a blanket around her lower half. "You could have mentioned I was half naked."

My roost mate stares at her in genuine confusion. "Why would I do that?"

She puts her hands on her face and groans softly, then lowers them again, her expression stern. "Because it's polite to tell someone if they're showing more skin than they realized. And we'll have to talk about where *I'm* ticklish, or we'll keep having this issue over and over."

I nod, appropriately chastened. "Certainly."

But Emmerich narrows his eyes at her. "What, you also wear clothes to the bathroom? Into the bathtub?"

Morgan opens her mouth, then shuts it again. She glares

right back. "Of course not. That's—that would be impractical."

"Aha!" Emmerich sits up, a triumphant grin lighting up his face. "So there *are* exceptions to the naked rule. All right. I will make it my mission to find out where else it's acceptable for you to be naked, *Liebchen*."

Then he's scrambling up, his wings flaring in his haste.

"Where are you going?" I ask.

I'd hoped for some more time in the nest. Perhaps we could reenact what happened last night—I've been hard for most of the night, thinking of how it would feel to finally lick Morgan's pussy like Emmerich did.

But he stands next to the nest, naked and hard, and puts his hands on his hips like an Army general. "We are going to have a bath."

"Are you *sure* this is big enough for all three of us?" Morgan eyes our bathtub warily.

"Not at all. We will remain outside of the bathtub for the moment," Emmerich says while he fiddles with the taps and tests the water pouring into our large clawfoot tub. Then he offers Morgan a sly look. "Unfortunately, you will have to bathe first. And we will have to wait and, uh, watch over you. Will that be a problem?"

Morgan, who insisted on bringing a sheet with her to the bathroom to cover her lower half, grins at him. "I'll live."

I'd dragged on my pants after leaving the nest because I didn't want my cock to bounce around while descending the stairs, but Emmerich had no such reservations. He's still naked, his ass flexing deliciously as he walks over to the dresser holding our towels. I want to move in and palm his cock, stroke him until he begs for more, but I want to see what his plan is. He seems to be on a mission, and I wouldn't want to cross his plans.

"Klaus?"

Morgan's voice pierces my distracted thoughts, and I turn to find her staring at me, eyebrows raised, like she has called my name more than once.

"Yes?"

"I only asked if you think I should use orange blossom or peppermint oil for the bath," she says, holding up two bottles she must have found at the edge of the tub.

I'd bought them months ago, hoping that our future mate would enjoy them, just like with the pillows and sheets in the closet upstairs. Since the summer, I've been drawn to acquire so many things in the human shops, things that had no real value for either Emmerich or me—but now it makes me wonder. Did I know ahead of time that our last mate would be human? Why else would I have bought so many warm blankets if not to keep her warm? Or these bathroom items I couldn't even tell apart?

"You choose," I rasp. "They're all for you."

Morgan's expression softens, and she sets both bottles back, then walks over to me, her sheet dragging like a train behind her. She doesn't stop until she's right in front of me, her brown eyes wide as she gazes up at me.

"What's wrong?" she asks. "If you're worried about the biting, I'm sure we'll figure it out."

I shake my head slowly, wondering how I should reply so that I won't reveal my innermost thoughts. "It's fine. Nothing is wrong."

She narrows her eyes at me. "Well, that's clearly a lie. Klaus… I don't have to smell you to know something's upsetting you. This—this *thing* won't work if we're not honest with each other."

Emmerich comes closer and puts his hand on my shoulder, squeezing. "She isn't wrong, you know. And I *can* smell you, so I know you're not telling us something."

It would kill me if Morgan rejected me because she was afraid of the biting—or being with a grumpy old gargoyle like me. It would be even worse if she accepted Emmerich and only wanted to be with him.

And perhaps that's the real issue here. They've formed such an easy relationship already, and meanwhile, I'm here, trying not to sink my teeth into my human mate's flesh instead of trying to woo her with *gentle* things like bath oils and fuzzy blankets.

Emmerich has the right idea, and I don't know if I can imitate him well enough. I don't know if I can prevent Morgan from running away, screaming—an event that wouldn't just hurt me but both of them as well.

I grit my teeth, grinding them together so hard my jaw hurts, and I keep my hands at my sides, not wanting to move too quickly and risk hurting Morgan.

They're asking *too much*. I couldn't possibly say all these things out loud.

Then Morgan bridges the gap between us and wraps her arms around my waist. Her sheet slips, and when I peer down over her shoulder, I see the rounded globes of her ass. My cock hardens in my pants despite everything—I want her, even if I'm not certain I should have her, ever.

"It's okay," she murmurs, her cheek resting against my chest. "You don't have to tell us now. Just tell me, do you want to stay here with us?"

I want to say no, but I'm physically incapable of lying to her. "Yes," I answer reluctantly. "But Morgan…"

"Then we'll start there." She speaks over me. "It doesn't have to be anything you don't want it to be. We can just relax and talk. After that, I'll need some breakfast because I'm hungry. Then we can try to figure out what to do next. Is that okay?"

My throat is inexplicably tight as I carefully put my arms around her and hold her close. She's tall for a human but still a head smaller than me, yet she fits perfectly in my embrace.

"That sounds nice," I tell her.

I can't say no. She is trying her hardest to understand us, and it means the world to me.

I glance up to find Emmerich watching us, his smile wry, a hand on his hip. I let out a deep sigh, and some of my tension melts away. Neither one of them are pushing me to speak, so maybe we can all forget about this awkwardness and move on. If I can get my strange thoughts under control, this could all turn out fine.

"Come on, the tub is nearly full," Emmerich prompts her after a moment.

Morgan lets out a sigh, squeezes me tight, then steps back, her brown eyes shiny. That sends another jolt of worry through me. Is she on the verge of crying? Humans cry a lot, and I'm not certain tears always mean deep sadness like with gargoyles, but what if she's still unhappy? I sniff the air between us but can't sense anything other than warmth and her relaxed, soft scent.

Huh.

It will take as much time for us to learn about humans as it will for Morgan to learn about us.

I won't rest until I know every single thing about her. How she takes her coffee. The kind of books she likes to read. The foods that bring a smile to her face and the films she enjoys. But most of all, I want to learn how to please her in every way, to show her how much joy we can find together.

"Right, I'd better get in." Morgan glances toward the tub. "I'm all sticky from last night."

I hum, my cock twitching. "I could lick it off you. If you don't want to bathe."

She flushes a deep pink, and I think I might have gone too far, but she stops in front of the bathtub and lifts her hands, indicating I should remove her t-shirt.

"All right, bathing it is," I murmur.

I put my hands on her waist, marveling at how different her smooth, golden skin is to my gray tone. Then I push the fabric up, exposing her perfect tits, which I had the pleasure of sucking last night. I don't tug her t-shirt off immediately but instead linger, cupping her tits with both palms. I run my thumbs gently over her nipples, watching in fascination as they draw in tighter, forming perfect little buds.

"Look how well you fill my palms."

My voice has gone guttural, too rough, but Morgan doesn't seem to mind.

She sways closer, her hands resting on my upper arms. "Klaus…"

I swallow thickly, then force myself to let go and do what she asked me to do. I draw her t-shirt over her head carefully so I don't dislodge her glasses, then take a step back.

Emmerich offers her his hand and helps her climb in. She gasps at the first contact with the hot water, then sits and leans back with an indecent moan.

My cock strains against my pants, so I press down on it, willing myself to hold it together.

"This feels so good," Morgan murmurs. "Exactly what I needed."

She lifts one long leg out of the water and rests the foot on the edge of the tub.

Realizing it's the one she injured yesterday, I draw closer, unable to stay away. "Does it still hurt?"

"No." She looks up at me, expression marveling. "That chutney thing really helped."

Emmerich crouches next to the tub, gently grasps her foot, and rotates it in slow, careful circles. "How does this feel?"

Morgan nibbles her lower lip. "Really good. I like it."

Emmerich groans, and I barely bite back an echoing sound—she is so responsive, so perfectly attuned to us, it's all I can do to keep my hands to myself.

But maybe I don't have to…

I kneel on the opposite side of the tub from Emmerich, right behind Morgan. She casts a coy look at me, then closes her eyes, leaning her head on the edge. From this vantage point, I have the perfect view of her wet body, her tits just under the surface of the water, her pussy hidden in the shadows between her legs.

My hands itch with the need to touch her, but I don't want to presume.

"Do you want Klaus' help with washing?" Emmerich asks suddenly.

I snap my gaze up to him, and he grins, his expression impish.

Morgan's lips turn up in a smile. "That would be lovely. Like I said earlier, I'm *very* sticky."

My hands tremble as I take a washcloth and wet it, dipping it in the water in front of her. Then I lean forward, bringing my cheek close to hers from behind.

"I'll have to touch you," I rasp. "To make sure you're nice and clean."

"You can touch me anywhere." She tips her head back to rest on my shoulder. "The water feels amazing."

My control is fraying, and she doesn't even know it. I glance up at Emmerich to see if he'll intervene, but he's still crouched in place, watching us, his eyes heavy-lidded.

I brush Morgan's damp, golden curls from her neck and run my nose over her shoulder, inhaling deeply. Then I take a bar of soap and rub the washcloth over it, creating a thick layer of foam. I move to the side of the tub to take Morgan's right arm and wash it thoroughly, from her shoulder to her fingertips, then flip it over and do the inner side as well, drawing a gasp and a giggle from her lips.

"Ticklish?" I ask, lifting one eyebrow.

"Yeah." She squirms but doesn't shift away. "I don't mind now that I'm anticipating it. You just surprised me earlier."

I hum to tell her I understand, then take another washcloth and toss it to Emmerich. He snatches it from the air and gives me a wide-eyed look, but I just nod at him to let him know that yes, I want him to help. He orchestrated this whole scenario, and he should reap the benefits.

And benefits they are—washing our mate is an almost sacred experience, especially since she seems to love it as much as we do.

He lathers up his washcloth and starts on her foot, resulting in more giggles, but I don't want to just watch, so I massage my washcloth over Morgan's neck and shoulders, carefully moving her hair out of the way. She gives me her glasses to set aside, then dips underwater and lets me wash her hair with one of the scented shampoos I'd gotten for her. Her little sighs are *everything*, and I intend to do this every day forever if she lets me.

By the time Emmerich starts on her other leg, Morgan is all but purring in pleasure, her scent so sweet, it's driving me mad. I've been avoiding her tits and the juncture of her thighs, as well as her ass, but when she bends forward to let me wash her back, I groan at the sight of her lush buttocks just outlined under the sudsy water.

"Gods, Morgan, you're a vision." I reach down into the warm water to trace the dip of her waist. "I never dreamed our mate would be this beautiful."

She lets out a quiet huff of breath. "Really?"

Emmerich nods vehemently. "It's hard to tell what my expectations were—they all faded from my memory the moment I saw you."

He runs his washcloth down her pale thigh, and she spreads her knees all by herself, giving him better access. But Emmerich, the tease, just grins and retraces his movements up her leg again.

"Klaus," she moans, shuffling back to rest her head on the edge of the tub.

I lean closer and cup her cheek with my hand. "What is it, sweet?"

Her calling my name while she's in the grip of lust is the best thing in the world. I want to hear it every day, want to hear her screaming it when I fuck her.

She shivers, then leans into my touch. "I want this."

Her whisper seems to pierce straight through the worries that have been plaguing me.

"You do?" I lick her neck, feeling as if I'll go mad if I don't taste her skin right now. "You'll have to tell me *exactly* what it is you want, Morgan. Or I might take everything from you. Because that's what I want. Every single piece of you."

Her gasp reverberates around the bathroom, but she doesn't move away from me. She doesn't try to escape or reach for Emmerich.

I'm running my hands all over her, from her belly to her tits, down her arms and to her soft, warm thighs. I want them wrapped around my waist as I fuck her deeply, but I'll take this, I'll take any bit of her she's willing to share.

Then I look up to find Emmerich grinning at me as if this is what he had planned all along. And maybe he had? I didn't know my mate was capable of subterfuge, but perhaps he *is* willing to manipulate me a little, to push me past my comfort zone.

"I want you to make me come," Morgan says, her voice

breathy but firm. "And I've been thinking… Now that you're still in control, do you want to try biting me?"

I freeze, my hands stilling on her hips, my mouth an inch from her skin. "What?"

Morgan cranes her neck to meet my gaze. "If you're afraid of letting go with me, we should practice. See where our limits are. I've never been bitten during sex, and you've never bitten a human. This is new territory for both of us, so we should do a controlled experiment."

I stare at her, blood pounding in my ears. "There's nothing *controlled* about what I'm feeling right now."

"I know you can do it. I trust you."

I glance at Emmerich to see if he's hearing this, but he seems to be well on his way to taking a nap judging by how relaxed he is. He's slowly massaging Morgan's foot, rubbing her sole with his thumbs, and I don't think he will help me with this.

It's my decision.

Morgan goes as if to move away from me—or maybe she just wants to face me fully—but I can't allow it. Now that I have her where I want her, I don't know how I'll let her go.

She smells so fucking good, I want to eat her, and I've lost all sense of propriety. Without thinking, I reach right between her legs and cup her pussy with my hand. It's so damn large compared to her, a monster's paw clutching at her, but Morgan doesn't seem to mind. She spreads her thighs and lets out a low moan. Her hands come up to clutch my arm, and it dawns on me that this is what she wanted all along.

Oh.

Glancing up at Emmerich, I find him smirking at me. Of course, he knew. I was so worried about hurting her or not fitting in, and all the while, they were waiting for me to get out of my own way and let my instincts take over.

I lower my head and graze my teeth from Morgan's shoulder to her neck, then follow the same line with wet kisses, tasting her. At the same time, I spread her lower lips with two fingers, then swipe my middle finger through her.

"There," she gasps, her chest expanding on a deep inhale. "That feels so good."

My entire body is primed and ready to fuck my mate, this beautiful human, but I'm holding on to this last shred of control. I can't do that yet, not until she comes at least once, and not in this bathtub. When she lets me into her body, I want her spread out in our nest, not squished in a small receptacle like this.

But I can definitely make her come without impaling her on my thick cock.

"What was it that you said last night?" Emmerich asks suddenly. "That Morgan and I looked good together? I can now say the same. I never thought I'd be this turned on by watching my mates pleasure each other."

I dip my finger lower, tracing the opening of Morgan's pussy. She's slick there, I can feel it despite the water, but the angle is wrong—I can't push my fingers into her and tease her like I want. Not without possibly nicking her tender flesh with my claws.

"Hmm." I roll my fingertips over her clit, enjoying her little gasps. "Emmerich, tell Morgan what you feel when I bite you."

He sucks in a breath, his wings flaring wide. "Oh, *Liebchen*, you will like it. Maybe just a nick for the first time, Klaus?" He looks up at me, his eyebrows high. "Just a tiny taste?"

I grin at him, pleased by his enthusiasm. I know he loves it when we fuck, and I can't wait to see how Morgan will fit into our roost.

"Explain it to her," I purr. "Tell her how hard it makes you come."

He groans, shifting in place, and I know he's itching to grasp his cock and stroke it—because I am, too.

He faces Morgan and reaches for her hand, then brings it up to his cheek, nuzzling into her palm. "When Klaus bites me, I feel him *everywhere*. Not just his cock but his spirit, connecting with mine." He glances up and gives me a small smile. "It's the purest form of love."

Morgan's eyelids flutter, and she lowers her gaze to her lap. "Oh. Then maybe I understand why you don't want to bite me yet."

I freeze, my hand cupping her pussy. "What?"

She squirms, but when she realizes I'm not letting go, she lets out a huff of exasperation. "Well, if it's *love* you need to bite me, I get why we're not there yet. It takes time. It's perfectly fine, and I don't mind at all."

Her words sound very reasonable, but her scent changes, a noticeable shift from sweet and turned on to embarrassment, bordering on…misery?

Oh, that will not do.

I press a kiss to her neck, then trail my lips to her shoulder, tasting her skin. She shivers, an instinctual response she can't hide from me—and I know she wants this.

She wants *us*, wants everything, but is afraid to ask. Whatever happened to her in the past to make her doubt herself, I will work all my life to undo it. To shower her with all the attention and love she needs, to protect her and satisfy her every whim.

"I want you on the verge of an orgasm before I sink my fangs in you," I murmur. "I've wanted it since the moment I saw you in the woods, Morgan. Never doubt that."

Emmerich is nodding, his expression radiating concern. "Yes, he is telling the truth. There is no need to wait, but we know humans don't bite each other. It's why Klaus is hesitating. What if you got scared and wanted to leave? We didn't want to scare you."

Morgan's beautiful eyes fill with tears, and she cranes her neck to look at me. "Is that true?"

I swallow thickly, my heart pounding. If I fuck this up now, she might still leave—and Emmerich will never forgive me. "It's true. I don't know if I could let you go. I would stalk you and keep you safe. I would kill any man who tried to put his hands on you. You're *mine*, Morgan, and I protect what's mine."

She's staring up at me, her breaths quickening. Goose bumps erupt on her skin despite the warm water, and my insides twist at the sudden fear that I've gone too far at last. That I said the wrong thing, even if it was the truth.

Morgan reaches up suddenly, grasping the back of my neck. She strains up and tugs me down at the same time, bringing our lips together in a violent kiss. She devours me, and I let her lead until she whimpers against my lips—then I take over. I tip her chin up and keep a hold of it to plunder her mouth, biting and licking like I've wanted to since the first moment I saw her. She's not holding back, so I don't either, and it quashes my fears better than any of her words.

She really wants this, and she's not afraid of us. She's not backing down.

Knowing this gives me the control I need. I break the kiss, grinning down at her. Her lips are pink and swollen from our kiss, her eyes hazy with lust. I drop another kiss on her mouth, then settle behind her like before, one hand on her pussy.

When I reach into the water with my other hand to cup her breast and pinch her nipple, Morgan relaxes back against the tub, her body relaxing. That's exactly what I want—I need her soft and distracted so she won't tense her muscles when I bite her.

She jerks lightly when I return to teasing her clit, but I just keep at it until her eyelids flutter shut, her lush lips parting. I jerk my chin at Emmerich to indicate he should help, and he takes her other ankle and digs his thumbs into the arch of her foot, drawing a moan from her.

I slide my fingertips lower, brushing the entrance of her pussy. Morgan brings her hand up to grasp my arm and hold on to it.

"Is that the spot?" I murmur in her ear. I lick the delicate shell, tracing the pattern with my tongue. "Is that where you want me, *Engel*?"

"Yeah." Her grip intensifies, and she sinks her blunt nails into my skin. "Right there, please."

"So polite," Emmerich rasps. "So fucking lovely when you demand to be fucked, Morgan."

She tips her head back, leaning on my shoulder where I'm pressed up against the tub. The position gives me an excellent view of her body—her tits bouncing with every move she makes, right at the surface of the water, her nipples drawn into tight points. But I want more, and it's getting harder and harder to hold myself back.

"Will you bite me when I come?" she asks, her voice breathless.

Can she read my mind? Maybe the mate bond works even more mysteriously than I'd previously thought.

"It will bind you to me." I force the words out before it's too late. "Complete the mate bond."

Morgan cries out and rides my hand, her slick body writhing against me. "I thought it was complete! I'm falling for you so quickly, I was sure that was it."

I snarl, the sound too feral, too wild. "You're killing me. You're everything we dreamed of, Morgan, and I want to make you mine, then watch as Emmerich bites you, too, so you'll never leave."

"Fuck!" Emmerich shudders, his big body curled over the tub. He's losing control as much as I am, and it's only a matter of time before he plucks Morgan from the bath and carries her upstairs to fuck her. "Klaus, *do it.*"

My mouth waters with the thought of tasting her blood, and my cock pulses with the need for release. I'm close to coming, even though I haven't touched myself yet—it's just *her*, wreaking havoc on me.

"Please," Morgan begs, writhing in the water. "I'm so, so close, Klaus!"

My exhale is a shuddering sigh. "How did we get so lucky? You're perfect. So curious. So brave." My voice comes out low, the final words I have to tell her heavy with meaning. "It's far more binding than human marriage, more permanent than any contract. If you think we're obsessed now, possessive of you, there's no limit of what we'd do for you afterward. And you'll feel the same about us. Once Emmerich bites you as well, we'll be able to feel each other, track each other by blood. Are you sure that's what you want?"

If I was a better person, I would wait to hear her answer when she's calm, not thrashing on the cusp of her climax. She could reject me—reject us—right now, and I would move away, but if there's a chance we'll get to keep her, I'm not throwing it away.

She opens her beautiful eyes and gazes right up at me. Then she breathes, "I'm sure."

Hope swells inside me, almost painfully intense. Emmerich lets out a helpless groan, kissing Morgan's leg, and I know he feels the same.

I give Morgan a nod because words have deserted me.

Then I return to my mission of bringing her to a swift, powerful orgasm—hoping that she won't regret this.

Nuzzling her neck, I brush aside her damp curls and choose the spot carefully—it will scar, a faint, silvery mark on her skin that will remain there forever, irrefutable proof of our bond. Not too high on her neck, even though I want everyone to know she's mine, but not too low on her shoulder, or my fangs could nick her bones. But there's a soft, fragrant spot between those that's just right.

I press a kiss there and soothe it with my tongue.

Then I sink my teeth into her skin.

CHAPTER 13

MORGAN

Klaus bites down on my shoulder, and the first flash of pain has me gasping, all my senses going on high alert. What the hell was I thinking, begging an apex predator to sink his supernaturally large fangs inside me?

Just as panic threatens to take hold of me, the pleasure hits, a rush of joy so powerful, my vision tunnels for a moment. My nerves, already stimulated by the pain, now flare with the most intense climax. Klaus presses down hard on my clit and shoves me over the edge.

But it's more than that—more than a simple orgasm, no matter how powerful. It's Klaus I feel, his essence thrumming right beside me, his life force surging through me.

I cry out, squeezing my eyes shut against the pulsing sensations. It's almost more than I can bear, and I'm sobbing and laughing at the same time, all while my pussy clenches around emptiness, needing to be filled. Klaus snarls, his growls completely feral, and twitches around me, his big muscles caging me in.

It's the most confusing sexual experience of my life, and I want *more*. Not because I've never come so hard I nearly blacked out but because I've never been this close to another person—Klaus is peeling me open, drawing my blood into his mouth and at the same time, laying himself bare, showing me his innermost being.

Tears streak down my cheeks, and I'm barely aware of Emmerich, who has come to crouch beside us, petting first one, then the other. He hums, and it's his touch that grounds me, bringing me back to earth. He seems to be doing the same to Klaus because the older gargoyle lets out a long sigh, then slowly releases my shoulder, his grip on me gentling.

The sensations that were so intense just moments ago still simmer in my belly, the awareness of Klaus' essence remaining even after he gently licks my wound and draws his hand from my pussy, resting his palm on my belly.

Huh.

Is this how it will be from now on? I keep my eyes closed for a moment longer, testing the feeling, trying to work out where he ends and I begin, but maybe we've become so completely entwined, we can no longer be pulled apart.

The thought should terrify me. I've willingly bound myself to a mythical creature I only met yesterday, but the realization of just how deep the bond goes doesn't bother me at all—on the contrary, an intense flush of satisfaction flows through me.

He's *mine*.

"Morgan?"

Emmerich's voice breaks the silence, so I force myself to open my eyelids, blinking to clear away my tears. Emmerich is staring down at me, his handsome face creased in concern. He cups my cheek and rubs his thumb under my eye to wipe away my tears, pauses—then brings his thumb to his mouth to suck the moisture off his fingertip.

I raise my eyebrows at him, amused, and his wings droop a little as if he's embarrassed by his actions.

"I'm good," I croak, my voice all scratchy from crying. "Um, this was intense."

Klaus moves into my field of vision. He's so damn beautiful, I don't know where to look—his straight eyebrows, currently furrowed in a frown, his firm lips, pressed together, or his magnificent horns that I want to grip and tug him down for a kiss. Finally, I settle on his gray eyes and see worry reflected there.

So I reach up and palm the back of his neck, even though I'm still limp from the experience. "I'm okay, I promise. You made me feel so good, but humans get tired after an orgasm." I pause, focusing on the glow inside my belly. "Hey, can you feel me inside you now?"

He nods, still not speaking. He wraps his big hands around the edge of the tub and grips so hard, his fingers leave indents in the metal.

I purse my lips and send him an admonishing look. I've grown quite fond of this tub, and I don't want him to rip it apart because he's worried about me.

"Try to focus on that feeling inside you," I tell him. "Does it feel like I'm agitated? Or can you tell I'm just completely blissed-out after you made me come so hard?"

He closes his eyes for a moment, obeying me. The corner of his lips turns up, and when he looks at me again, there's an unmistakable smugness in his expression.

"You enjoyed it," he states.

"I did," I agree. "More than I thought. And you didn't hurt me."

Emmerich leans in close. "It didn't hurt? At all? I didn't know humans were so resilient."

I put my hand over his, stopping him. "It did hurt a little at the start." I speak quickly so Klaus doesn't get worried again. "But it was very brief and well worth the pleasure that came after."

They don't seem *entirely* convinced, but hopefully they will be by the time we do this next and I beg them for their bites. I want Emmerich's especially—now that I can feel Klaus like this, I want it with Emmerich, too. As soon as possible.

Glancing down at my hand, I wince at how pruney my fingertips are. "I'd better get out, I've been in here long enough."

Emmerich's eyes flare with alarm. He takes my palm and traces his fingers over it, prodding at the folds of skin that are so normal for me, but apparently not for him.

"What happened?" he demands. "Is the water hurting you? Klaus, she's disintegrating!"

I gently pull my hand from his grip. "I'm not. This is how human skin gets in the water. It helps us grip on to things underwater."

Emmerich plucks me from the tub regardless of my assurances and wraps me in a large, fluffy towel. Behind us, Klaus is washing in my bathwater, which could be weird but somehow isn't—and he does need it, since he apparently climaxed right after me, only he'd still been wearing his leather pants then. It must be super uncomfortable for him, but I feel a little smug, knowing I wasn't the only one affected by his biting.

I'm pretty sure my panties and bra are still upstairs, next to our nest. I snag my t-shirt from the floor and give it an experimental sniff, then grimace. "Yikes. You guys don't own a washing machine, do you?"

Emmerich tilts his head to the side. "How do you think we wash the bedding? And our towels?"

I flush, embarrassed. "Well, you did a very good job convincing everyone this tower was abandoned. I was surprised to learn you had running water, let alone electricity."

"We are civilized," he tells me, his expression somber. "And I will wash your clothes if you let me."

"That's okay, just show me—" I start to say, then shut up at the sight of his frown.

Maybe I should just let him take care of me?

It doesn't come easily, giving up this much control over my life. It's not just about the clothes either—I literally cannot leave this tower without their help. If I tried, it would be a very long drop from the roof, and I'm not a fan of that idea.

For better or for worse, I chose them, which probably means I'll have to…adjust a little.

Before I can assure Emmerich that I'm more than happy to let him wash my stinky clothes, he tightens the towel around me and scoops me up, too quickly for me to even protest. I let out a yelp, unable to move my arms, but he just laughs and gathers me closer to his chest.

"I like carrying you," he confides as he climbs the stairs. "You're a perfect armful. And you smell so nice."

He carries me from the bathroom all the way to the top floor of their tower. My bare legs press up against his leathery side. The tips of my toes brush his left wing, and it twitches open, and I wonder if I gave up on my tickling test too soon—maybe it's his wings that are the most sensitive. I want to explore more of him, find out everything that makes him different from a human—and from the way he's staring at me, I think he feels the same. His grip on me is secure, and he rubs his thumb over the naked skin on my shoulder, the gesture so small it seems instinctual, but when I glance up at him, he gives me a broad, wicked smile.

This gargoyle knows exactly what he's doing.

The main room of their roost is toasty warm, though not

stuffy. Emmerich must have added more wood to the fire because it's blazing. He sets me down gently in the nest of blankets and pillows in front of it.

"We must dry your hair." He fingers the damp strands with care. "Wait here."

He disappears back down the stairs, leaving me sitting in my nest with only a towel wrapped around me. Klaus, who must have finished washing downstairs, walks slowly to his armchair and sits, his gaze on me. We stare at each other, and I wonder how we'll proceed now that we have this full-fledged connection between us. He must have had a change of clothes downstairs because he's in a fresh pair of pants, dark denim this time, and he looks *delicious*, sprawled in the armchair, his wings fanning out on either side of him. He doesn't even blink, he's so focused on watching me, and I stare right back, studying his stunning form.

This is the moment when you wrap yourself in blankets, Morgan.

Even if we aren't going to do anything sexual right now, it's not exactly proper to be sitting in a man's living room, wearing nothing but a towel.

But I don't move. Because Klaus' gaze tracks from my eyes to my lips, then trails down to where I'm holding up the towel. His chest expands on a deep breath, and the vein in his neck throbs faster, testifying to the fact that he's affected, too.

Footsteps on the stairs announce Emmerich's return, and I snap my gaze over to him, embarrassed to be found staring like that. But the younger gargoyle only grins and sits behind me, his massive wings flopping on the floor on either side of us.

"You smell delectable, *Liebchen*," he purrs. "I am glad you find Klaus so attractive."

The gargoyle in question drags his palm over his face in

an exasperated gesture. "Emmerich, must you say everything that comes through your head?"

Emmerich shrugs, unrepentant. "Why shouldn't I say what is true?"

I hide my grin behind my palm, cheeks heating up. "Um, most humans aren't really used to saying things like that out loud."

Emmerich produces an intricately carved wooden comb and reaches for my hair. His touch is gentle as he teases it through my tangles. I try not to shiver at the touch of his warm fingers on my neck and shoulders. The rhythmic tug and slide of the comb has me closing my eyes in pleasure.

"I am not human," he says at long last. "But I will try to keep that in mind if you want me to."

My heart skips a beat at his words. He's so unique, so perfect, that I don't want him thinking he has to change himself in any way.

I turn in the nest, facing him, and take his wrist to stop him. "I don't mind," I say honestly. "It might take me some time to get used to it, but I like how straightforward you are."

Emmerich's dark eyes light up. "Does that mean I can tell you I want you to drop your towel so I can feed my cock into your pussy and show you how well I can take care of you?"

Behind me, Klaus lets out a choked sound.

My face flames, but I force myself not to look away. "You *can* tell me that," I reply, my voice higher than before. "That doesn't necessarily mean I'll do it."

Emmerich tilts his head to the side and draws in a big inhale through his nose. "But you want to, yes? I can smell it on you."

Okay, so maybe Klaus had a point, and having Emmerich declare what he can scent on me isn't the best idea.

I clear my throat. "I'm not saying *no* to your idea, and I do want it, but I think I need a little break. I'd like some breakfast and maybe a chat before we try *that*."

Emmerich's eyes widen in horror. "Morgan! Why didn't you remind us that you need food?"

"It's okay, I'm not going to starve if I don't eat immediately…"

I try to reason with him, but he's already on his feet, pulling me along and marching into the kitchen, still buck naked.

"Klaus," he yells over his shoulder, "come on, we have to feed our human!"

CHAPTER 14

MORGAN

Klaus stops Emmerich from hand-feeding me protein bars and coaxes his worried roost mate to let go of me so that I can put on a shirt he offers me. It's long enough to cover my ass, very wide in the shoulders, and has slits in the back—for the wings. But it does the trick and lets me feel a little less exposed. I put my towel over a chair near the fire to dry, then root through the food that Arielle and her new kraken boyfriend sent for me.

Then we sit in front of the fire, warm pieces of toast over the flames, and I get both of them to try peanut butter and jelly sandwiches for the first time. Predictably, Emmerich loves them and demolishes two before he stops himself, looking guilty for eating my food, but Klaus scrunches up his nose and declares that peanut butter is vile, coating his mouth.

I only remember it's Christmas when I take my phone off silent mode and see my mom's unanswered call.

"Oh, wow, I forgot," I murmur, curling up in the

armchair. I glance back at the guys to find them watching me closely. "I have to call my parents. Is that okay?"

I'm not exactly sure why I'm asking. It's not really permission I need. I could go out into the stairway for some privacy, but I don't want Klaus and Emmerich to think I'm hiding something from them. Then it occurs to me that I can't do a video call because my mom and dad would see the tower room, which would lead to questions about where I'm spending my Christmas—and with whom.

"Of course," Klaus says smoothly. "Come on, Emmerich, let's give her some privacy."

Emmerich hesitates, then moves away, and they settle on the couch, talking quietly. Guilt gnaws at me at the thought of keeping them a secret, but we haven't talked about this yet —and as much as I want to trust my parents, there's no way I'm telling them about the supernatural community until I get the green light from the guys.

"Hi, sweetie," my mom chirps as she answers the phone, then yells, "Robert, come quickly, it's Morgan!"

I hold the phone away from my ear, cringing at her loud voice. "Hey, Mom, sorry for not picking up. I forgot to switch off the silent mode this morning."

"It's fine," she says. "We only called to say Merry Christmas and to ask how you're doing. Did you have a good time last night?"

I think hard, trying to remember what exactly I told them —then it comes to me. "Yeah, it was good to spend some time with Arielle. We had a nice dinner."

"Honey, how much snow did you get overnight?" Dad asks. "You need any help shoveling the driveway? I could come up when the roads clear a bit…"

I imagine him leaning over Mom's shoulder, his face creased with concern.

"Um, several inches for sure," I tell him, "but it's fine. I saw a couple of neighborhood kids making the rounds with shovels, I'll pay someone to help me if I can't manage on my own."

"You could ask that neighbor of yours," Mom says, her voice turning sly. "You said he was good-looking."

"Stacy," Dad admonishes.

"What?" Mom goes on the defensive. "*She's* the one who said he was handsome. I'm just worried, Nick. She's all alone, hours away from us. I'm her *mother*. Am I not allowed to worry about my daughter?"

I cover my eyes with my palm, holding in a sigh. "I'm fine, Mom."

"I'm sure you are, Morgan. But you're supposed to be better than *fine*. You're young, baby. You're supposed to be out with your friends, doing wonderful stuff, being carefree, and falling in love." She pauses, then adds, "And I know we said we wouldn't press you about your breakup, but it's been months. Don't you think it's time to move on?"

At the gentleness in her voice, my throat closes up, and I glance at Klaus and Emmerich, sitting on the couch. They're both staring at me, still as statues, and I realize they've stopped pretending that they're engrossed in a conversation of their own—and they're likely listening in on my conversation.

Embarrassment wells up in my chest, a dark swirl of emotion. Now they'll know that I've been so pathetic, my mother is seriously worried about me. Am I ready to move on? Before coming here, I distracted myself with work, then following the lead Arielle told me about—the story of mythical creatures haunting an abandoned tower. Now that this mate bond had snapped in place between Emmerich, Klaus, and me, I feel amazing, but before I met them, I wasn't in a good place. I put myself in danger by traipsing through the woods in a snowstorm just to *feel* something—and to stop myself from thinking of how miserable my life had become.

Am I even in the right state of mind to start a new relationship? What if I'm being massively unfair to Klaus and Emmerich, promising them things I can't deliver on because I'm still stuck in the past? Maybe our connection will fizzle out like everything else in my life, and they'll see through the pheromone-induced bliss to the real mess that's hiding underneath.

"Morgan?" Dad's voice comes through, concern radiating through it. "Are you still there?"

Now both gargoyles are frowning at me. Emmerich's nostrils flare, and he tenses, his big body primed to spring forward. But it's Klaus who stands first and walks over to stand in front of me.

"Yeah," I croak. "I'm okay, I promise. I'll—I'll come visit soon."

My mom's sigh is shuddery, as if she, too, is holding back tears. "I'm sorry, sweetie. I didn't mean to say all that out loud."

"It's all good," I force myself to say, struggling to keep my voice level. "I miss you."

At that, Klaus suddenly swoops down and yanks me into his arms. A moment later, I'm being carried across the living space and straight into the nest, so I clutch my phone to my ear and grasp Klaus' arm to keep from pitching to the floor. But he holds me safely and hands me off to Emmerich, who is already kneeling in our nest of blankets, somehow still naked. He settles me in his lap, his wings flaring out to create a canopy around us. Then Klaus is there, huddling close. He wraps his arms around me and squeezes lightly, then settles at Emmerich's side and takes my feet into his lap. He kisses the sole of my left foot gently, then massages the spot, his warm touch so comforting. Emmerich puts his chin on top of my head and rumbles quietly, as if everything is all right in the world now that I'm back in his embrace.

It's only then that I remember my parents and realize Mom is still speaking, her voice tender.

"…love you so much, baby, we just want you to be happy."

I clear my throat, some of the pressure in my chest lessening. "I love you, too. But you don't have to worry about me. I'm okay. In fact, I met someone new."

A pause from the other end has me smiling—I can picture Mom and Dad exchanging surprised glances, communicating wordlessly. They're one of the lucky couples who met in college and fell so deeply in love, they've been together ever since. Dad still brings my mom flowers every week, and she blushes every time, thanking him with a kiss. It's adorable—if a little difficult to watch when my love life hasn't been this great.

But all that is changing now. Emmerich and Klaus are right here, and even though this is all still so new, I know it's built to last. The glow in my chest tells me as much. Klaus' presence is currently stronger than Emmerich's due to us sharing that bite, but I know it'll grow into a balanced, steady love.

"You have?" Mom asks tentatively. "When?"

"Just recently," I admit. "It's still a very new thing, but I have a good feeling about it."

Emmerich squeezes me closer to his chest. The warmth of his naked body permeates through the thin fabric of my borrowed shirt, and that helps, too. Klaus gives me an approving look, his gray gaze soft.

"That's great, honey," Dad says. "Is he treating you well?"

"Yeah," I say immediately. Then I take a deep breath and add, "They both are."

Now Klaus full-on smiles at me, and my breath catches in

my throat. He's so handsome, I can't believe I thought he was a demon when I first saw him.

"B-both?" My mom's voice turns squeaky. "Oh. That's nice, Morgan. Uh, when will we get to meet them?"

I press my lips together, fighting a grin. I told them about my *two* mates because this is actually the lesser of the surprises—eventually, I'll have to tell my parents that Emmerich and Klaus aren't human. But we'll work on that.

"We'll see. Like I said, this thing is still pretty new, but I'll tell you more when we see each other next, okay?"

"Okay," Dad says quickly. "As long as you're happy, we're happy. We love you very much, like your mom said."

I get the feeling he's speaking up so Mom doesn't pepper me with more questions.

"Thanks, Dad. I love you, too, and I can't wait to see you soon."

We say our goodbyes, and finally, I end the call and set the phone down. I take a moment and just breathe, leaning on Emmerich's chest, and neither of my gargoyles forces me to speak. They seem to know I need it, and they don't pry, somehow sensing my mood better than anyone ever has.

"I'm not hung up on my ex anymore." I glance up at Emmerich. "I swear this isn't some rebound strategy. I genuinely l-like you and want you and I'm serious about making this work."

I stutter over my words, because something else tried to force its way out my mouth, but I don't think any of us is ready for those important words just yet.

Emmerich nods, his beautiful eyes serious. "I know. I feel it in you." He pauses and brushes my hair away from my face, studying me, then adds, "I don't think you would have connected with us so easily if you still had feelings for someone else."

Klaus circles my ankle with his large hand and gives me a

firm squeeze. "And I feel your emotions through the bond, *Engel*. You are hiding nothing from us, and I respect that so much."

I chew on the inside of my cheek, one question still bothering me. "You don't think I'm pathetic?"

Emmerich rears back, frowning at me. "Pathetic? Why?"

I shrug, trying to make it seem like it's no big deal. "Because my parents are so worried about me." I pause, then force myself to tell the truth. "I was pretty sad about the whole breakup thing. It got to a point where my parents were really worried about me because I couldn't get off the couch some days, but I worked through it." I lift my chin, defiance surging through me. "I went to therapy and got my life together. It's not much—my apartment or my job, I mean—but they're enough for me."

Klaus hums deep in his throat. "We would be pathetic, Morgan, if we judged you for mourning a relationship lost. You are strong, and I am glad for whatever happened in your past because it brought you right to us."

Emmerich is nodding vehemently, his chin bumping the top of my head. "Klaus speaks for both of us, as always. I'm sorry you were in pain, but you ended up here, so hopefully, it will all be worth it in the end."

I sniffle as a wave of relief crashes over me. I wrap my arms around Emmerich's broad chest. "It already is."

He rumbles out a laugh, his hands going to my waist. "What do you want to do now? Are you hungry again? You haven't eaten in a while."

My sweet gargoyle, always taking care of me.

"I'm all right for now," I tell him. "What would you be doing if I wasn't here?"

They exchange a look, and Emmerich shrugs, then jerks his chin at Klaus as if to pass the question to him.

"We would be resting," Klaus says. "Cleaning the tower,

hunting, reading by the fire. We'd just finished our last assignment the day before you arrived, and we don't have anything scheduled until after the New Year."

"Ooh." I squirm in Emmerich's lap, curiosity flaring up. "Were you guarding anything important?"

"As a matter of fact, we were," Klaus says, his smile turning smug. "But I'm not sure you're ready for a revelation of this magnitude."

He's teasing me, but it's totally working.

"You can't say something like that and not tell me." I bat my eyelashes at him.

Emmerich lowers his head and whispers into my ear, "It was the sea dragon king from Norway and his witch queen. They spent a week here in Boston, meeting with the local coven, and needed a neutral party to watch over the negotiations."

My eyes bug out, and I stare at him, unsure if he's joking or not. "A-a dragon? There are *dragons*, too?"

"A sea dragon," Klaus corrects me. "Though there are some regular dragon clans still living in Europe, but they're not very fond of witches. They were all involved in several bloody wars over the last century and a half, and the witches nearly eradicated the dragons. Hence the need for negotiations and enhanced security."

Wow. I have so much to learn. I want to ask them about so many things, but I also don't want to treat them as walking, talking encyclopedias, so I swallow my questions for the moment.

"Can I stay with you tonight, too?" I ask instead. "I was planning on spending the holidays alone, but I'd rather be with you."

Klaus leans close and touches his forehead to mine. "If you think we'd rather send you away to stay close to your handsome neighbor, you're mistaken."

It takes me a moment to remember what my mom said during our call. "Oh my God. My neighbor isn't even that handsome. He's younger than me and can barely speak up when I say hi to him, and besides, I only told mom he was handsome because she *asked* about him. I mean, I guess he's objectively good-looking, but he's not my type at all." I realize I'm babbling, so I snap my mouth shut and offer Klaus a sheepish grin. "Anyway, you have nothing to worry about. So if this is your only reason for keeping me here…"

"It's not." His eyes glow with a banked fire, his powerful will tightly reined in. "Tell me, Morgan, what *is* your type?"

I squirm in Emmerich's lap, trying my best to ignore his growing erection pressing up against my thigh. He must be scenting me—my belly is warming, my heartbeat picking up, and I know it's only minutes before I'm slick and ready for them. It's the effect they have on me, and it's good to know that they're equally turned on.

"I guess it's guys with very large…wings," I say, purposefully drawing out the pause. "And horns. I've been really into horns lately."

"Hmm." Emmerich slips his palm under the edge of my shirt. "How do you feel about tails?"

"Love them," I breathe. I think of how he used his to make me come just last night and barely hold back a sigh. "Tails are surprisingly great."

Klaus puts his hands on my knees, and I let my thighs fall open, my instincts taking over. He shudders, then draws in an inhale, and I know he's scenting my pussy, which is getting wet in anticipation of whatever they have in mind for me.

"That's good," Emmerich says, his large hand splayed on my belly. "Because *my* type is tall human women with golden curls and beautiful brown eyes. I'm especially interested in those who have a habit of walking through snowy forests alone."

I can't hold back a moan when he slips his hand lower, brushing over my mound, so close to where I need him but still too far. "That's great to hear. So cool that our interests align."

Klaus watches us, his focus intense. Then he purposefully closes my thighs and moves away from me.

I whimper, then flush, embarrassed at the needy sound, but *damn* him for pulling away right when I thought we'd take another step together.

"What are you doing?"

He offers me his hand, palm up, looking very gentleman-like, even though he's still shirtless and no Victorian gentleman ever sported such impressive muscles, let alone wings, horns, and a tail.

"It's Christmas," he says, smirking.

Emmerich hums but doesn't stop me from putting my hand in Klaus'.

"What do you have in mind?" I let Klaus pull me to my feet and straighten my borrowed shirt. "I didn't think you guys celebrated human holidays."

"We didn't until now," Klaus confirms. "But we have a human mate, and we want to make sure you're not deprived of *any* experiences."

I'm about to protest and say that they don't need to make a fuss out of this. I'm not a kid anymore, and I don't mind not having a big celebration. I like Christmas as much as anyone, but I'm not about to demand they change their habits because of me.

But Emmerich jumps up, his wings carrying him a step farther than us because he's so excited. He smacks his hands together and asks, "Where do we begin, Morgan? What do humans do for their Christmas?"

I think about my family's traditions. A lot of them won't be feasible because of where we are at the moment, snowed in and essentially trapped here in the middle of the forest. But surely there's something we can do...?

"We will make a list," Klaus declares. "But first, Emmerich should put on some pants."

CHAPTER 15

EMMERICH

I sit on our couch, Morgan in my lap, and stare down at the list we put together. We have already put up a string of twinkle lights—something I'd picked up on a whim when shopping for nest materials. I'd thought it would make for nice, cozy lighting, but Morgan was delighted to string the lights along our mantelpiece, even though she said she might move them to the tree later.

We also lit a truly extraordinary amount of candles, setting them on all windowsills and tables, put on some Christmas music on the radio, and researched German Christmas traditions because Morgan wanted to include something from our motherland.

When we told her that one of our dear friends was a Krampus and we could pay him a visit soon, her eyes got very round, and she nervously declined. I didn't quite understand that because he is very friendly, but perhaps she got scared of the images she saw on the internet, which aren't true at all. Our friend, Dominic, is quite kind and makes

Christmas tree ornaments, so I think she will like him when she gets to meet him.

She doesn't seem to mind that I'm touching her all the time, and I try to do it subtly, but my need is still burning bright. I want what Klaus has already—the soul-deep connection with Morgan.

I see how it has affected them, too, even though they might not have noticed it themselves. Klaus was so grumpy earlier, casting glances at Morgan and me, almost as if he resented how easily she accepted me. And Morgan was wary, still unsure of her place with us, in our roost, but now all that is gone. They gravitate towards each other, subtly shifting their ways to interact more.

And I'm being selfish right now, keeping Morgan in my lap, I know it. But for now, she doesn't seem to mind because she's distracted with planning our Christmas Day. I hope I will get to give her my bite tonight, but the last thing I want is to rush her. She has accepted Klaus', yes, but that doesn't mean she wants mine so soon after. Perhaps her skin is still tender. I caught her touching the bite mark several times already. Maybe it hurt her more than she admitted to us and she won't want to repeat the experience.

At that thought, a rumble starts in my chest, growling I can't quite keep down. Morgan blinks and glances up at me, her focus broken.

"It's nothing," I say gruffly, not wanting to admit I've sunk to a deep, dark level of my mind. Instead, I nod at the list in her hand and ask, "What should we do first?"

Morgan hesitates for a moment, as if she wants to press the issue, but I swallow thickly, and the growling stops. *There*. That's better.

"I think we need a tree first," she says at last. "There's no use in us making ornaments if we don't have anywhere to hang them. And maybe we could get some boughs for the mantelpiece as well?"

Klaus nods immediately. "What kind of tree do you want?"

Morgan shrugs. "Um, any type of conifer will do. A small one, so it doesn't take up too much space. A pine, maybe, or a spruce?"

I can get my Morgan a tree. If she wants it, I will deliver it.

But first, I need a goodbye kiss.

Taking Morgan's chin, I turn her face gently and kiss her full lips, taking care not to bump her glasses with my horns. I love how she melts for me, her tongue darting out to meet mine, allowing me to get a taste of her. But I pull back before I can get carried away, then take her waist and set her on her feet.

"I'll be back soon," I declare, marching toward the door. "You will have your tree."

"Wait, don't you need more clothes?" Morgan calls after me.

I send her a smirk over my shoulder. "I am a gargoyle, *Liebchen*. This is exactly what we love."

With that, I leave her to Klaus' care, even though it pains me to walk away from my mates. But I will return with everything she wants—and more.

Because I have a plan, and I intend to surprise my human with more than just the tree.

Sneaking downstairs instead of up, I open the storage room where Klaus and I keep our human clothes, as well as the glamour charms we buy from Irma. I slip on a shirt and a jacket, not to protect me from the snow but to keep the humans from staring at me too much, then put on a charm necklace. The magic pours over me, and I shiver. Letting someone manipulate my exterior is always uncomfortable, even though we trust our witchy friend.

I check the mirror hanging on the wall and brush my hair from my forehead. Staring back at me is a scowling human man, tall but unremarkable, with brown hair and blue eyes, dressed in very human-looking clothes. My horns have disappeared, as have my wings. I wrap my tail around my waist to keep it from smacking into random passersby, and then I'm ready.

I tiptoe upstairs, hoping Klaus is sufficiently distracted by the Christmas music humming from the radio—and by Morgan, of course. Their voices filter through the door. My heart pangs at the sound of Morgan's laughter, and the need to return to her side is so strong, I'm reaching for the doorknob without even realizing it. I stop myself just in time, though, pulling back and squeezing my hand into a fist.

I will do this first, make sure my Morgan isn't disappointed in her first Christmas with us, and show her I will provide for everything. Whatever she might wish for will be hers.

With careful footsteps, I climb the stairs to the rooftop terrace. The wind that meets me is frigid, but I take a deep breath, letting the cold air clear my thoughts and fill my lungs. Snowflakes swirl through the air, landing on my shoulders and glamour-hidden wings, but they don't bother me at all. This is what we were made for. To protect and to provide for our mates.

One last glance at the staircase tells me I got away clean. No one is coming after me, and I have some time now to carry out my plan.

So I take a running leap and throw myself into the storm.

CHAPTER 16

MORGAN

"He's been gone a long time."

I glance toward the window, watching the snow drift down in big flurries. The sky is still overcast and seems intent on dumping out the largest amount of snow possible. It's dark, even though it's early afternoon, and I'm beginning to worry about Emmerich. He left more than an hour ago, and we haven't heard from him since.

Klaus looks up from the paper star he's been painstakingly cutting from cardboard. He's been making Christmas ornaments with me for most of the time since Emmerich's departure and hasn't complained once, even though this can't be his favorite way of passing the time.

"I'm sure he's all right," he says, his voice a soothing rumble. "He is a gargoyle. We're used to harsh weather."

I return to cutting out a large cardboard heart. Firelight flickers over our table setup. I don't think Emmerich and

Klaus would keep the tower room this warm if it was just them in residence, but ever since Klaus saw me wrapping myself in a blanket to fight off the chill, he's kept the fire burning bright. I try to focus on my task—we've only cut out enough ornaments for a very small tree—but something's still bothering me.

"How long does it take to find a tree in a forest?" I burst out, setting down my scissors and cardboard. "He should have been back by now. I have a bad feeling about this, Klaus. What if something happened to him? Just because I sent him out for a stupid Christmas tree…"

Klaus slowly cuts the last arm of his star, then puts it on the stack of ornaments in the middle of the table. Only then does he look up, his eyebrows furrowed. "That's a good point. I could go out to search for him, but he could be anywhere on our property now, and visibility is very poor. And I'd be leaving you alone here at the tower, which Emmerich would never forgive me for."

I jump to my feet and hurry over to the window, anxiously peering outside. "We could go together. You can carry me. Then you won't have to—"

"Absolutely not," Klaus snaps. He stands, his hands on his hips. "This is not weather meant for humans."

I get his point, but he's being unreasonable. "I have my snow gear," I remind him. "It's dry, and I can spend *hours* outside if I wrap up well."

He stills, watching me intently.

"If we're going to have an *equal* relationship, you're going to have to let me do *dangerous* things sometimes." I keep my voice low and calm. This is something we have to agree on, or we'll never work. "And you'll have to trust me that I know my limits better than you do. You might think I'm weak because I'm smaller and softer than you, but humans are pretty resilient."

His throat bobs, and he lowers his wings, a sure sign he's calming down. Then he walks closer to me and takes my shoulders, squeezing lightly. "Forgive me. I don't think you're weak—and I trust you implicitly. But we only just found you, and I couldn't live with myself if anything happened to you."

"I get that," I agree. "Which is exactly why I'm worried about Emmerich and want to go with you."

Klaus lets out a long sigh. "All right. But you'll put on *all* your clothes, and I'll wrap you in blankets before we leave. If I think you're staying out there just to prove how tough you are, I will fly you home immediately, so you must promise to tell me if you're nearing your limits. Agreed?"

"Yes."

I offer him my hand, smiling despite my worries. He compromised, even though he could have easily overpowered me and exerted his will.

Klaus reaches for my hand and shakes it, his expression solemn. "Get ready, then. We'd better start soon, or we'll lose all the light."

I throw myself toward the door, where my snow gear is hanging on a hook, put there by Emmerich this morning. He'd tidied it up, thinking I wouldn't need it for days, maybe, but now I do—and I don't like this one bit. What could have happened to a gargoyle to keep him away from his roost for so long?

My mind flashes to the weather first as I drag on my thermal layer and socks. Maybe he got blown off course by the wild winds and crashed somewhere? Or a tree fell on him, burying him under the snow?

With shaking hands, I button up my snow pants, then sit to lace up my boots, but I'm too anxious to do it right, so I have to do it again, and it all serves to ratchet up my worries even higher.

Because what if it's not nature he's battling against? What

if he was *seen*? By a human? By a hunter who would have mistaken him for a demon, perhaps, and shot him on sight? Or maybe…

"Morgan?" Klaus crouches in front of me, his forehead creased with concern. "What is it? You smell so nervous."

I look up, my eyes welling with tears. "I'm just *worried*, Klaus."

He squeezes my shoulder. "Come on. We'll find him. There's no need to worry yet."

A thud has us both jerking to attention, our gazes flying to the door.

"Wait here," Klaus barks, already striding for the door.

I don't even bother disagreeing with him—I run after him, my still-untied shoelaces trailing behind me. In the stairway, a cold draft blows down from the roof, meaning the door upstairs must be open.

"Emmerich?" I call, climbing the stairs behind Klaus. "Is that you?"

Another *thump*, and my belly swoops with fear—if he's not answering, he could be hurt! What if he only made it to the tower, then collapsed…

Klaus bursts through the half-open door onto the roof. A stream of muffled German follows before I push the door open, too, and find myself on the frozen rooftop landing space, knee-deep in snow.

And there is Emmerich—or a dark-haired man I assume is him, wearing a glamour—kneeling and clearly unwell, his hair and clothes crusted with ice and snow, his body shuddering from exertion. I've never seen this version of him before, but I *know* him, my soul recognizing him as the gargoyle I've come to—

"Oh my God!" I rush forward and fling my arms around his neck. "What happened? Are you hurt?"

He reacts slowly and puts his arms around me. "*Hallo, Liebchen. Mir geht es gut.*"

"English, please," I murmur against his chest, though I think I understand what he's saying. "But you can tell me downstairs. Come on, we have to get you out of this cold."

He groans and stumbles to his feet, and Klaus swoops in to support him. My relief at his return is short-lived, because Emmerich stumbles, pitching forward, and when I rush in to help him, his wings, still invisible, are ice-cold to the touch. What if he got frostbite flying in this weather?

I hurry forward and hold the door open for Klaus, who half carries Emmerich down the stairs.

"Wait," Emmerich croaks. "Don't forget the things!"

I'm trying to get past them to open the door to the living room, but there's not enough room in the stairwell. "What things?"

Emmerich lifts his head, a smirk lifting the corners of his lips. "I brought Christmas."

I exchange a look with Klaus over Emmerich's shoulder. *He brought Christmas?*

"Okay." I keep my voice calm despite my growing worry. "Let's get you warm first, and then we can see about your things."

He lets Klaus drag him to the armchair by the fire, and I set to brushing the snow and melting ice off his wings and shoulders, working by touch alone. When he leans back against the armchair, a strange pendant slips from under the collar of his shirt.

Klaus reaches in and snatches the amulet from Emmerich's neck, tearing the string. "Why wear a glamour? Did you fly all the way to town?"

The real Emmerich appears in all his monstrous glory, gray-skinned, winged, and a little sheepish.

"What?" I tug at Emmerich's horn. "But that's at least ten miles away! What on earth were you thinking?"

He takes my waist and pulls me closer, until I'm standing between his knees. "I wanted to give you a Christmas to remember. With all the good food and presents."

Klaus drags a palm over his face. *"Meine Götter, Emmerich, was hast du dir dabei gedacht?"*

I can't be sure, but from the exasperation in his voice, I think he's asking him what the hell he'd been thinking.

Emmerich juts out his chin, his expression stubborn. "Morgan deserves a good holiday."

"But it *is* good," I cry. "I didn't want you to hurt yourself over this."

He pulls me even closer, and I end up sitting on his knee, my hands pressed to his chest. He's damp and cold all over, but I don't care—I'm just glad he's okay.

He brushes a slow kiss over my lips, then touches his forehead to mine. "I'm sorry I worried you. I should have told you where I was going."

"Yes, you should have," I grumble. Then I shove at the sodden jacket he must have put on to pass as human. "Take this off. You need to get dry and then we'll warm you up in the nest."

Klaus steps closer. He takes Emmerich's face between his hands and tips it up, then kisses him fiercely. "I will get your things from the roof. You must do exactly as Morgan says."

Emmerich's smile turns wicked. "I won't say no to that."

I groan. "How can you be thinking about sex when you nearly froze to death?" I peel the jacket off him and hang it on a chair to dry. "You know what? Never mind. There will be no sex until your temperature is back to normal. You're cold as marble. That can't be good, even for a gargoyle."

He meekly allows me to remove his shirt as well, then

gives me a sly look. "So you are saying that there *will* be sex once I'm warm again?"

I smack his shoulder with the back of my hand, instantly regretting it when my knuckles bounce off his stone-hard muscles. "Ow! I still haven't forgiven you for scaring us." I point at my snow pants. "We were getting ready to fly out after you. Klaus didn't want to leave me here alone, so he agreed to carry me while we went searching."

Emmerich sobers immediately and catches my hand, then presses a kiss to my aching fingers. "I'm sorry, *Liebchen*. Will you believe me if I promise you I'll never do that again?" He shudders, then shakes out his wings, sending droplets of water flying all over the stone floor. "I hope you will like your present."

I melt at his concern. "I'll like it no matter what. But you didn't have to get me anything."

Taking the towel I used that morning, I scrub it gently over his wings. He shivers and twitches as I dry them, one joint and membrane at a time. His breathing turns ragged as I close in on the biggest joint at his shoulder blades, so I linger there, pressing down to test his reaction.

"Morgan…"

His low growl has heat pooling in my belly—it seems my body has forgiven him, even if I'm still holding out the judgment.

The door behind us opens, and I whirl around to find Klaus there, his arms laden with bags—several of them. I have no clue where Emmerich got all that on Christmas Day, and in a full snowmaggedon situation. They must have been buried under the snow when we ran up to the roof, because they're damp and dripping water everywhere, and so is Klaus, who must have spent some time searching for them all.

All that pales in comparison to what he's dragging behind him.

"Oh my God, you got us a tree?" I drop the towel on the armchair next to Emmerich and rush forward. "And, uh, you brought the whole thing, roots and all?"

The tree—a small fir, judging by its needles—is covered with snow, its branches frozen and stiff, but it's already shedding bits of branches and bark all over the floor. It's larger than any tree we ever had at home with my parents, and certainly bigger than my fake Christmas tree I set up a couple of weeks ago in my living room.

But Emmerich brought it for me, so it's the best damn Christmas tree I've ever seen, even though it's unconventional and has a root system still attached.

Klaus lifts one eyebrow as if to say, "You asked for this, you deal with it."

I grab the tree trunk and drag the whole thing into the middle of the living room. My palms scrape on the rough bark, but I don't complain because Klaus is right—this was my idea, and I need to figure it out. But there's an issue I haven't thought of, and it might just ruin everything.

"Morgan?" Emmerich calls from the armchair. He's leaning forward, his elbows on his knees as he holds his wings out to dry by the fire. "You don't like it?"

"No, it's great," I say, then pause and nibble on my lower lip, wondering how to explain what's wrong. "I forgot that we need a tree stand."

"A tree stand?" Emmerich asks, slowly straightening.

I motion at the tree. "Yeah, you know, to put the tree up. It-it can't stand on its own." I glance around the room, searching for a solution. "We *could* just lean it against that wall, I guess…"

Emmerich's wings droop dramatically. "So we won't have a nice tree after all?"

I rush toward him and settle right back in his arms to comfort him. "No, it'll still look lovely, I swear. We just have to chop off the roots and let it thaw out, and then we'll figure it out."

Klaus, who has been watching us all this time with his hands at his hips, lets out a sigh. "Wait here."

Then he stomps out of the room and disappears from sight.

"He's not flying out, is he?" I ask, worry swamping me again. "Because we've had enough frozen gargoyles for one day."

"No, I can hear him moving around downstairs," Emmerich says.

Then the door opens again, and Klaus stands there, a ball of string in one hand. "Let's see what we can do to fix this."

CHAPTER 17

MORGAN

An hour later, the world outside is dark, though the wind still howls around the tower. But in our cozy living room, the fire blazes bright, and our first ever Christmas tree is up, decorated with homemade paper ornaments.

"It's the most perfect tree I've ever seen," I declare, meaning it. "Thank you for doing this for me."

Klaus wraps his arm around my shoulders and pulls me into his side. "You don't think it's too...rustic?"

He motions at the jagged end of the tree stump, where he simply wrenched away the root ball because they didn't have a wood saw in the tower. The move showed me just how powerful Gargoyles really are—he didn't even scrape his palms. But he did get tree sap on his leather pants, which we'll have to fix sometime soon.

"I genuinely like it," I tell him. "We can make homemade ornaments every year. Or keep these in a box so we'll always have the ones we made for our first Christmas together. But maybe it would be better to get a tree from a farm or something. Not sure if uprooting trees every year is sustainable for our forest."

Klaus' expression gentles. "*Our* forest. I like the sound of that."

I widen my eyes, a brief surge of anxiety flaring up. "Sorry, I didn't mean—"

"Of course you did. You belong here, Morgan. We are very happy to share our forest with you."

My throat closes up, and I have to swallow twice before speaking. "I've never had a forest before."

"It's yours to explore." He brings me closer to press his lips to my forehead. "As is the tower."

I grab his arm and squeeze, digging my fingernails into his skin. "Does that mean the bat colony is *also* mine?"

"Yes." Klaus' rumbling laugh fills the living room. "I've never seen anyone as excited about bats before. Are all humans like that?"

I think of Arielle, who shrieked like a banshee the one time I took her bat watching with me, and a very small flock flew right at us when we opened the shutters of an abandoned house on the other side of town.

"Uh, no, that's just me," I admit. "Most people think they're creepy, what with vampires turning into bats and all."

He goggles at me. "What?"

"You know." I motion with my hand. "Count Dracula? He's a book character and he can turn into a bat."

Klaus shakes his head in disbelief. "The things humans cook up. Vampires don't turn into bats, *Engel*."

"Wait." I squint up at him. "You're saying there are actual vampires? Like—"

"Like gargoyles and dragon shifters, yes," he says patiently. "There aren't very many of them left, but one of the witches from Boston who we've worked with is mated to one. Very decent guy. Obsessed with his mate."

I remain quiet as my inner beliefs about this world reorganize themselves again. Vampires and witches, gargoyles and dragons. And kraken, let's not forget about those. What I thought was a local legend turned out to be reality, and I'm not entirely sure I've completely come to terms with that. It seems so improbable—especially since I haven't actually seen any of the other supernatural beings, just Emmerich and Klaus.

I gaze up at Klaus, who's still contemplating the Christmas tree, his heavy, warm arm slung around my shoulders. *They* are real. So very solid and present. So the rest of what they told me must be true as well.

Following Klaus' gaze to the Christmas tree, I let out a deep breath. I guess I'm up for a steep learning curve. I can't stop the smile that stretches my lips. This is going to be so much fun.

Just then, Emmerich bustles into the room, his wings out and angled so his arms are hidden.

"Don't look," he commands, shuffling sideways, his back to us. "It will spoil the surprise."

I giggle but nudge Klaus so we both turn away from him, then call out, "We're not peeking." Then I realize Klaus is craning his neck to peer over his shoulder, so I grab his horn and tug lightly. "Come on, no cheating."

After some huffing and the sound of scrunching paper, Emmerich finally announces, "I'm ready. You can look now."

Anticipation rises in me as Klaus drops his arm from around my shoulders and turns on his heels. I follow suit—and find myself staring at Emmerich, who is standing next to the Christmas tree, bouncing on the balls of his feet. His wings are open, the ends twitching lightly. He is so excited for this, my heart swells with love for him—he went out of his way to prepare this surprise for me, and I already know I'll adore every moment of it.

"What do you have there?" Klaus points at Emmerich's feet.

I was more focused on three badly wrapped parcels under the tree, but now that Klaus mentioned the bag, I'm curious as well.

Emmerich's grin is wide as he bends down to pick up a large paper shopping bag from a local twenty-four-hour grocery store. I've shopped there before, mostly on the weekends at about ten in the evening, when I needed something chocolatey to get me through the melancholy of living alone so far from my family.

"I brought Christmas food," Emmerich announces. "I hope it will be enough for tonight. The nice lady at the cash desk told me they are open tomorrow as well."

I take the bag from him and huff as it weighs down my arms. It's heavier than anticipated, and it's a wonder that it held out at all, what with all the damp and snow. I carry it over to the dining table and peer inside.

"I hope you like cake," Emmerich says, hovering behind me. "But I got other food as well, just in case."

I take out a cake in a plastic box. It's a small one and says *Merry Christmas* on top and is decorated with tiny fondant snowmen. It's slightly squished on the side where it must have moved during the flight, but I shake the box lightly, and it doesn't seem too badly damaged.

"This is great," I tell the gargoyle leaning over my shoulder. "I love the decorations."

He beams at me, then motions at the bag. "There's more."

The next thing is a dish with six heavily frosted cinnamon rolls, which Emmerich bought because they apparently smelled good to him. Then there are cookies in the shape of Christmas trees, a bag of mini marshmallows, which reminded him of snow, and—randomly—a box of instant noodles, which he got because it had a Santa printed on it. I pull out a bag of apples—"You liked the apples human Arielle sent to you, *Liebchen*"—as well as a can of green beans with bacon and maple syrup.

At that, I arch my eyebrow at him. "Do gargoyles like green beans?"

He frowns at me. "No, but the lady said humans like to eat them for Christmas dinner. She said they might go nicely with the steak I bought." He reaches into the bag and brings out a large bag of meat, several packages all neatly vacuum-sealed. "She asked me if I had anywhere to cook the meat, and I said of course, we have a fireplace."

I pull my lips in and swallow the bubble of laughter trying to escape me. "That was nice of her. Um, Emmerich? What exactly did you say to her?"

He shrugs. "I saw the meat in the fridge, so I got some for Klaus and me. Then I thought that maybe you would like some, as well, but I didn't know if you liked to eat just meat for the main course or not."

"I don't," I tell him. "That was good thinking."

Klaus raises his eyebrows at me and looks like he might say something, so I nudge him with my foot and shake my head subtly. This isn't the moment to educate Emmerich on human interactions.

"Yes, I wanted everything to be perfect." Emmerich smiles again. "So I asked the lady what humans usually eat with meat, and that's how we got to the beans. Oh, and the potatoes. There has to be a bag somewhere…"

He roots through the bottom of the bag and pulls out a plastic bag of potatoes, his expression triumphant.

"Perfect," I tell him. I take the bag of potatoes from him, then wrap him in a big hug. "Thank you for thinking of me. We'll have a Christmas feast tonight."

I don't say that I will do the grocery shopping from now on—or at least accompany him to avoid raising anyone's suspicions. I wonder what the cashier thought about the strange man who wandered into the shop on Christmas Day, asking such questions. But then, knowing Emmerich, he was likely very polite about it all and made her day.

"Do you want to see the presents now?" he asks.

I release his waist. "I do, but I was wondering…"

He raises his eyebrows at me, the corners of his lips tipping up. "You want to see the bats now?"

I return his smile. "How did you know?"

Klaus swoops in and kisses my cheek, then nudges me toward my snow boots at the door. "You've only mentioned them about half a dozen times."

I open my mouth to protest, then close it again because… he's right. I *did* do that—and they're not annoyed. Instead, they're leaving the cozy warmth of the living room and heading out into the cold with me just so I can look at some hibernating critters.

If this isn't love, I don't know what is.

I grin at them and quickly push my feet into my boots, forgoing socks for the moment. We climb the staircase together, and I try to contain my excitement, but it's just *too cool*, having a whole bat colony right here. I leap onto the roof, my boots sinking into the snow, and look around for access to the attic.

But Emmerich shakes his head and pulls me back into the stairwell, then shows me a smaller door, its hinges rusty and covered in cobwebs.

"We don't disturb them often," he murmurs. "We only come here every once in a while to clean out their droppings."

I bounce on the balls of my feet. "I'm ready."

Emmerich opens the unlocked door, pulling it wide for

me. The musty smell of animals, poop, and dust hits my senses, and I rub my nose to prevent myself from sneezing. The last thing I want to do is scare the poor hibernating bats and have them fly at me in a confused rush.

It takes my eyes a minute to adjust to the low light, with only a sliver coming in through the door from the stairwell. I search the darkness above me for the familiar shapes—and then I notice the first cluster, several plum-sized shadows hanging quietly from a beam.

"*Oh.*" I shuffle closer, taking care not to trip over the boards or step into piles of droppings. "There you are."

As my vision improves, I see more and more of the bats, some hanging out in the open, their brown wings wrapped tightly around their small bodies. But most have chosen narrower hiding places, perching between walls and roofbeams, or behind old boards and unused window shutters.

"Such a cozy place for you," I croon, lifting myself on my tiptoes to study a cluster of maybe forty bats. They twitch lightly from time to time, proof that they're alive and breathing. Come spring, this place will be buzzing with activity, especially at night, and I can't wait to experience that.

I turn on my heels to find Klaus and Emmerich standing at the entrance to the attic, waiting for me. They didn't enter the attic, probably because it's narrow, and they'd disturb the bats with their loud footsteps.

The enormity of this situation hits me then. My massive gargoyles, protecting a whole colony of these small creatures... They could have chased them out, closed up the attic by attaching wire mesh to the vents and windows, and prevented them from returning. Instead, they clean out their dung, keep the attic well ventilated, and leave them to roost in peace.

Tears well in my eyes, and I wipe my palms quickly over

my cheeks to wipe them away. Then I tiptoe out of the attic and close the door behind me.

"What's wrong?" Klaus frowns down at me. "Did the bats upset you?"

I let out a wet laugh, shaking my head. "No, they're perfect. I think they're *Myotis lucifugus*, little brown bats. Big brown bats are actually more common in Maine, but these guys are too small to be them."

Emmerich cups my cheek with his large palm and swipes his thumb under my eye. "Why are you crying, then?"

I let out a shuddering sigh. "Because you two are the best. I don't ever want to leave here." I let myself show them all the happiness bubbling inside my chest. "And before you claim I'm only doing this for the bats, I want to say that for once, they have *nothing* to do with this. It's all you."

"Thank you," Emmerich says, his voice solemn. "You are the best, too."

Klaus' gray eyes glimmer in the low light. "We've been waiting a long time for a mate, Morgan. And every single day of that wait was worth it—for you."

CHAPTER 18

MORGAN

We return downstairs together. I would have stayed with the bats a little longer, but Emmerich noticed I'd started shivering and scooped me up in his arms before I could protest. He carried me downstairs to the warm living room, and Klaus followed, his gaze fixed on me.

The things we said to each other at the top of the tower are still ringing in my ears, the truth of how I feel about them settling somewhere deep inside me. It might be fast, it might be mad, but that doesn't mean it's not *right*.

Emmerich sets me down and brushes a kiss on my lips, then finally releases me so I can remove my boots and wash my hands of the dust I'd collected in the attic.

Then he puts himself right in front of me and announces, "It's time for the presents now."

I gaze up at him, affection warming my belly. "You didn't have to get me anything."

But he just guides me gently to the Christmas tree. "I got presents for *all* of us. I visited the apothecary."

Klaus lets out a huff of laughter. "Was Irma's shop open?" He turns to me and adds, "She's, ah, she can be a little scary sometimes."

A witch who *gargoyles* think is scary? She must be formidable.

"No, but I knocked on the back door, and she opened it for me," Emmerich explains, oblivious to Klaus' words. "She said she was happy for us when I told her we found a mate. Wants us to bring Morgan around to the shop so she can meet her in person."

"That's lovely of her." I do my best to keep the trepidation from my voice.

Emmerich takes the first present from under the tree. It's tiny in his big hands, and he holds it with care. "Here, this one is for you. It has two things in it."

"Don't tell me." I hold up a hand to stop him. "I want it to be a surprise."

I peel open the paper and find a box roughly the size of my palm. It's white and has no labels on it, so I shake it lightly, trying to figure out what he got me.

"Open it," he prompts me.

I lift the top of the box and stare down at the two pieces of jewelry in shock. They're beautiful, made of silver, and each of them holds a gemstone. One is a necklace with an amethyst pendant, and the other a bracelet with a smaller green stone.

"They're gorgeous," I breathe, looking up at Emmerich. "Thank you."

He plucks out the necklace and holds it up for me. "I only wanted to get this one. It is a fertility charm, you see." He shuffles his feet, seeming suddenly uncomfortable. "But when Irma heard we only found you so recently, she insisted I get this one as well."

He points at the bracelet, his nose scrunching up.

"A fertility charm?" My voice goes squeaky as I study the necklace, thinking of all the implications. "Emmerich…"

"Yes, yes," he says, his wings drooping. "I know. It is too soon to be thinking of our future brood. That's what Irma said as well. This green stone holds a contraceptive charm. She said to come by before the full moon every month to get it replenished, but it should keep you from getting pregnant, even with two strong gargoyle mates."

I don't know Irma yet, but I have a feeling we'll get along great. It's not that I don't appreciate Emmerich's necklace, but he's right. It *is* too soon to be thinking of babies.

"Thank you." I take the amethyst necklace from him, then hug him tightly. "I'm not saying no to children. But I want to get to know you two first. Is that okay?" I crane my head back to meet his gaze and add, "I will keep it safe until it's time to put it on. And then I'll gladly wear it every day."

He nods, his expression solemn. "All right. You will have to tell us when you're ready. We will not rush you."

Klaus steps closer and wraps his arms around me from behind, putting me in a gargoyle sandwich. "Emmerich is right, we won't. But know that we will both be very happy to make children with you." His hands travel down to my hips, and he gives me a firm squeeze. "*Anytime* you want."

My heart thumps harder at that, and I have to bite my lip to hold back the crazy ideas that want to roll off my tongue. Ideas that would start by me putting on the amethyst pendant instead of that pretty bracelet and end with a tower full of tiny gargoyle babies.

"Oh," Emmerich groans, then buries his nose in my hair, curling down to sniff at me. "Your scent is changing."

I squeeze my thighs. "Is it?"

Klaus shuffles closer, so I'm pressed between them, our bodies touching shoulder to knee.

Emmerich lets out a rumbling purr, but just when I think he might give in and carry me to our nest, he steps back, his chest heaving with deep breaths. "Wait. There are more presents."

"Okay." I put my palm over my eyes, trying to calm myself. "I can do this."

Klaus chuckles, his breath brushing my temple. "What's wrong, Morgan?"

I turn in his arms, then pinch his arm lightly, though I can barely make a dent in his thick skin. "You know what. We're all dancing around the issue of what happens next and I…" I pause, not sure how to continue. "I've never been with a supernatural guy before. Or two guys at the same time. This is all new to me."

Klaus lifts his hands and puts them on my cheeks, holding me so gently. "I know. And we've never been with a human, so this is new territory for all of us. We'll figure it out together."

"This will help," Emmerich says from next to us, offering a present for Klaus.

This one is roughly cylindrical in shape, but it's been wrapped in so many layers of paper, it takes Klaus a while to gently pry apart the wrappings.

"I didn't want it to break," Emmerich explains. "It's quite fragile."

I lift my eyebrows at this, but when Klaus undoes the last layer, and a glass bottle of a clear liquid slides into his palm, I can't say I expected this.

"Irma assured me it's safe for humans to use." Emmerich takes the bottle from Klaus, uncaps it, and pours a little dollop of the liquid into Klaus' hand. "It warms the skin and helps with friction, is what she said."

Oh, Irma, you amazing witchy godmother.

"It's lube, isn't it?" I ask. "I love it. We'll need plenty of it, I think."

Klaus rubs a finger through the liquid, his posture tense. Then he frowns at me. "We would not fuck you if you weren't ready for us, Morgan. If you weren't wet with pleasure and very willing."

"Oh, no, that's not what I meant." I take his hand and splay my fingers out against his to show him how much smaller my palm is than his. "I've seen Emmerich's cock, Klaus. I assume you're, ah, similarly blessed?"

"Of course," he grumbles. His eyebrows draw together, and he looks very fierce for a moment.

"Well, if you want to put your monster cock anywhere near my pussy, we'll need all the help we can get." I grin up at him. "I'm excited, but I'm also terrified. This will ease my mind. Does that make sense?"

"Hmm," is all he says, but he takes the bottle from Emmerich, caps it, and sets it in the nest.

All right, then. I'll take that as his agreement.

I face Emmerich again. "What's the last present? What did you buy for yourself?"

He walks to the Christmas tree and takes the last present. It's very thin and light, as if he'd only wrapped a gift card or an envelope.

He hands it to me, his expression hopeful.

Careful not to tear anything, I slip my finger under the tape and pry it open, then unfold the paper. Inside is a printed receipt, and I glance up at Emmerich to confirm that this is, indeed, what he wanted to present to me. At his encouraging nod, I scan the lines of the receipt. There's a logo on top with what could be a sporting goods store—judging by the silhouette of a cross-country skier—and lower on the page is…

"A tandem harness?" I frown and flip the page over, trying to find more information. "What's that?"

Emmerich's smile shines brighter. "I asked Irma how we could fly with you, and she said some humans take a parachute and jump from a hill or a plane, but together." He takes my hips and turns me around, positioning me so my back is flush with his front. "Like so. But they have a sort of harness system to tie themselves together so one of them doesn't plummet down and die."

"I didn't know this existed." Klaus plucks the sheet of paper from my hands. He scans it, then sends Emmerich an accusatory glare. "You only bought one?"

Emmerich sidesteps around me and wraps Klaus in a tight embrace. "There is only one Morgan. I thought we could share it. Irma said she might not like it at all, but I know she will." He turns back to me, so hopeful. "Won't you?"

I think of how safe I felt in Klaus' arms when he flew me from the forest to the top of the tower. It *would* be much better if I knew I was also held up by sturdy, human-approved nylon straps.

"Yeah," I agree. "I think I'd like to try."

"Excellent." Emmerich pounces at me, grabs me by the waist, and lifts me in his arms. "I will fly you anywhere you want, *Liebchen*."

I put my legs around his waist and hold on tight—but the position gives me a naughty, possibly dangerous idea. "Do you think the harness would work if I was facing this way?"

Emmerich tilts his head to the side. "But then you wouldn't be able to enjoy the view as— *Ohh*." His eyebrows climb higher. "Oh, yes, I'm sure we can make it work."

Klaus snorts, folding himself around us once again. "Promise me you won't try it alone. I want to be there in case Emmerich forgets to fly in the throes of his climax."

A giggle escapes me, and I bury my face in Emmerich's neck, inhaling his clean, wintery scent. "We'll have to practice lots. Before we attempt sex midair, I mean."

Emmerich pulls back and stares down at me. "Are you certain? We don't have to do this just because I bought a harness."

I shake my head, smiling. "It's not just because of that. Or because you brought us magic lube or the extremely cool contraception bracelet. I just want to. With you and with Klaus."

He doesn't waste any time—he simply turns and takes several quick strides to reach our nest. There, I expect him to lay me down and climb over me, but he doesn't seem capable of letting me go at the moment. He sits, then scoots back, still keeping me firmly anchored to his front. His erection pokes me from below, hidden by the leather of his pants, and I try not to squirm too much, even though it's *almost* in the right place for me to…

"Oh," I gasp when he hoists me closer, bringing my pussy right over his cock. My leggings are too thin to provide any real barrier, and the sensations are amazing. "This already feels good."

He palms my ass with big hands, squeezing my cheeks. "I've never been with a woman. Or a human. But your pussy was so wet when I licked you last night. Are you wet now?"

"Yeah." I dig my fingers in his thick hair and give him a firm tug. "But we have to do one thing first."

I glance over my shoulder to find Klaus standing at the foot of our nest, the silver bracelet in his hand. He smirks at me, and I know he can feel the desire thrumming through my veins just as clearly as I can sense his. This bond thing is amazing. I want to revel in it and soak myself in his emotions, but right now, we're both too excited.

"Forgot something?"

He kneels beside us and offers me the charmed jewelry. It looks so dainty in his palm, and when he tries to put it on my hand, his big fingers are no match for the tiny clasp.

"Wait, I'll do it." I reach to take the bracelet from him.

He palms my cheek, his rumbling echoing around the room. "So eager. So perfect."

I flash him a quick grin, then show him how to hold one end of the bracelet so I can clip the clasp in place. The bracelet settles on my wrist, the silver cool and just snug enough.

"Huh." I peer at the green gemstone closely, expecting to find…something. But it's just a regular stone, no visible swirls of magic inside. "I don't feel any different."

"This is Irma's charm," Emmerich says. "It works."

I lift my eyebrows at him. "You're that sure of her?"

"She does our glamours," he tells me. "They hold fast for hours, and no human has ever recognized us. She has a sterling reputation, and she would rather eat glass than sell a shoddy charm."

"All right, then."

My grin is a little wobbly because—holy shit—this is *it*. This is the moment when I have penetrative sex with *two* gargoyles, and while I am definitely all in, I also saw their *equipment*, and I'm not sure I'll be able to walk tomorrow.

But Klaus seems to sense my anxiety, because he moves behind me and reaches for my waist. He slips his palms under my borrowed shirt and caresses me, the warmth of his hands so soothing, my shoulders relax and I let out a deep exhale.

"We do this slowly," he murmurs, his lips skimming the skin on my neck, sending shivers down my spine. "All right? We have all the time in the world, and we need to make sure Morgan doesn't get hurt."

I'm nodding along—but at his last words, I glance at

Emmerich, who is staring up at me with a solemn expression.

"If you think it would be safer for you, I can get the chains from the basement," he says, completely serious.

I freeze, my hands on his chest, where I'd put them to explore his magnificent muscles. "What? Why do you have *chains* in the basement, Emmerich?"

Klaus' exhale warms my skin. "Are you imagining a torture chamber?"

I shoot him a glare over my shoulder. "Kind of? I mean—he said *chains*. In the *basement*."

His handsome lips turn up in a smile. "Yes. But they're very modern chains, spelled to be strong enough to hold a gargoyle—or a werewolf, for that matter—in place."

I hiss as his knuckles skim the underside of my breasts, then move lower again, always soothing. "Okay, but *why* do you have them?"

"Because Emmerich likes to be tied down sometimes," he murmurs in my ear. "He enjoys it when I chain him to those hooks over there and fuck him hard while he can barely move."

I follow the line of his finger to the wall, where a pair of heavy-duty steel hooks have been drilled into the stones.

Then I glance down at Emmerich, whose expression I can't quite discern—until I realize he's embarrassed. Humans usually flush when they're feeling unsure, but gargoyles don't, so he just seems abashed, his gaze somewhere on my midriff, his wings and tail twitching lightly.

"Hey." I lean down and press a kiss to his cheek. "That's nothing to be embarrassed about. I enjoy a lot of things that other people might find strange."

And if he wants to be tied down sometimes, I can already tell we'll have loads of fun. My belly warms at the thought, my pussy clenching around emptiness.

God, I hope this will be as good as I think it can be…

Emmerich lifts his chin at that, his beautiful blue-gray eyes wide. "Like what?"

I grin, sensing his interest. "I like to have my nipples pinched hard. The pain really does something for me—but I don't like being spanked. I don't mind being held down, and I can take it pretty rough when it comes to actual sex. Apparently, I also like oral combined with tail action. What you did last night was *amazing*."

Emmerich's cock twitches underneath me, and we both look down at the bulge in his leather pants. He groans softly, and his hands join Klaus' on my body. He grips my thighs and rocks me over his cock in small thrusts, his hips moving in time.

Klaus slides his hands higher and finally, finally, he cups my tits, his big hands perfectly sized to hold me. When he brings his thumbs and forefingers to my nipples and pinches them just like I said, my mouth falls open on a gasp.

"Fuck, you smell good." He drags his nose over my neck, inhaling deeply. "See, Emmerich, she is right. We will learn what we like and how we can fuck each other so we're *all* getting exactly what we want."

My eyelids flutter shut at the perfect pressure he's putting on my nipples, so I roll my head back to rest it against his shoulder. "What do *you* like?"

He hums, and for a moment, I think he might not answer —that maybe he prefers to remain mysterious.

But he puts his lips to my ear and murmurs, "I like watching you two together. Last night, you both did so well. But I will also enjoy holding you down, *Engel*. I'll enjoy fucking Emmerich while he fucks *you*, and feeling his ass clench around my cock as he comes in your tight pussy."

My entire body reacts to his words. I shudder uncontrollably, and when he increases the pressure on my nipples, I'm surprised to feel the first tremors of a climax building inside me. It's just that Emmerich is teasing me so perfectly, the ridge of his cock exactly where I need it, and Klaus' filthy promises are pushing me higher.

I whimper and dig my fingernails in Emmerich's skin. He groans, then surges up to kiss me. He's demanding, devouring my mouth with bites and licks. He sucks on my lower lip and gazes down at me with such heat, I know he must be just as turned on as I am.

Then he leans *over* my shoulder and kisses Klaus, their mouths meeting in a hard, uncompromising kiss. Emmerich's grip on my hips intensifies, and he thrusts up, meeting me in a perfect surge. Klaus groans into his mouth, his eyes closed—and it's so fucking hot, seeing him lose himself like that. I can't tell if he can sense how close I am, but he squeezes my tits harder, his claws digging into my soft skin.

My orgasm is swift and potent, rushing through me in a blinding wave of pleasure. I moan and shudder between them, rubbing myself all over Emmerich to chase those delicious sensations for just a moment longer.

The gargoyles both freeze, their hard bodies caging me in. For a moment, silence reigns in the room, the only sounds the crackle of the fire and our labored breaths.

Then Emmerich lets out a booming laugh that echoes around the tower room. He cups my face with both hands and kisses me, and I can feel his grin against my lips. I smile right back, my body still pulsing with the aftershocks.

"Oh, Morgan." He flops back onto the pillows and stretches his arms over his head, the picture of sinful power. "I didn't expect you to come so soon."

My cheeks must be flushed, and I'm sure my panties and leggings are soaked between my legs. "Yeah, well, I can't help it. You two were doing all the right things."

Klaus slowly releases my tits, though he caresses them first to soothe any pinch of pain. I want to protest—I don't want him to stop touching me—but he just moves to the buttons on the shirt. He undoes them one by one, even though he could rip the thing open, and it builds my anticipation of what's to come.

"Can human women come multiple times in a row?" Emmerich asks, still lounging there, his arms tucked behind his head. "I wanted to be inside you when you came. I've never had a pussy squeeze my cock."

I push back my messy hair and lean back to give Klaus room to work. "We can. It's not exactly common, but it's medically possible."

I've never been one for multiples—but whether that was my fault for not trying or my partners' for being satisfied with just one, I have no idea. But I want to try. With them. If anyone can make me go off like that twice, it's Emmerich and Klaus. I've never been this attracted to anyone before.

"I like a challenge," Klaus murmurs as he undoes the last button. He slips the too-big shirt off my shoulders and tosses it to the side, then kisses my naked shoulder. "If you want to stop at any time, just ask."

Goose bumps erupt all over my skin at his touch. "Deal. Now it's my turn."

CHAPTER 19

MORGAN

I reach for the waistband of Emmerich's pants, and he lets me undo them and lifts his ass to help me pull them off. When his cock springs free, I stare at it for a long moment, worry flaring inside me again. Is it possible it's even bigger than yesterday? What the hell have I been thinking?

But then Klaus touches me again, urging me to lean forward so he can remove my leggings and underwear, and soon, we're all naked in the nest together, skin sliding against skin as we shift against each other. Every kiss feels so damn good, my fears are slowly melting away—and I get it. It's the endorphins from my orgasm, combined with the fresh arousal. Whatever this mating stuff is doing to me must be affecting my gland system as well, preparing me to have sex with my gargoyles.

When Emmerich tumbles me over to my back, I stretch out underneath him. Klaus lies down beside me and props himself up on one elbow, looking so much like a Greek statue. Emmerich settles between my thighs and flares his wings wide, then closes them around us, a canopy of gray, though the edges of the membranes are so thin, firelight filters through, allowing me to see *everything*.

"You're stunning," I tell him.

I run my palms up his chest to his muscular shoulders. I press my thumbs onto his nipples, and he hisses in a breath, then lowers himself to suck my tits. My body arches off the bed, and I let my knees fall wider to accommodate him better.

"I can't wait," he rasps, lifting himself over me. He kisses me once, twice, then rears back and grasps his thick cock. "Tell me I can put my cock inside you, Morgan."

I laugh, breathless. "Yes to that. Please. I-I promise to tell you if it'll hurt too much."

His beautiful eyes flare with heat as he closes in and fits the head of his cock to my pussy. He runs it up and down, coating himself in my juices, and when the very tip hits my clit, I suck in a quick inhale.

"Oh, you like that?" He repeats the move, slipping down to my entrance, then up again, teasing. "Don't worry, I will take care of you."

"I know." I grasp his horn with one hand and pull him down for a kiss. "I trust you."

Those words seem to break some wall of resistance inside him. Emmerich lets out a low growl, then notches himself at my pussy and pushes slowly. My body clenches up on instinct—because I didn't realize how large he really is. I saw his dick and *knew* he'd have trouble fitting inside me, but feeling him there…

"Wow." I squirm, trying to let him in, but all that does is make his cockhead slip away, bumping my clit again. "Sorry, sorry, let's try again."

If we can't make this work…

Before my thoughts can take an anxious turn, Klaus leans in and kisses me, his tongue sliding languidly against mine. I close my eyes and let go, relaxing under his touch. He palms my cheek, then moves his hand to my throat and holds me there, squeezing gently.

My body lights up like a Christmas tree. The contrast between his strength and the reverent way he's holding me, combined with the knowledge that he could easily break me in half is doing something to my hindbrain, putting me in a state of mind I've never experienced before. I…let go. I said I trusted Emmerich, and I do, but now that I can feel Klaus' assurance pulsing through our mating bond, I *know* everything will be okay.

I relax completely, and between my legs, Emmerich lets out a long groan as his cockhead slips inside my pussy. The intrusion feels foreign for a moment, but when he pushes inside a little more, it morphs into the most wonderful sense of fullness. The strange ridges and bumps on his cock worried me before, but they feel *amazing* dragging over my G-spot, so I tip my ass higher to chase the sensations. He pulls out almost completely and slides back in.

"Oh, fuck." I moan and clutch his shoulders. "You feel so good, baby."

"Hold on," he rasps. "I'm almost halfway in. Just—stay still for a bit."

I freeze at that and stare down my body to find him feeding more of his large cock into my pussy. I tighten around him instinctively—because *no way in hell* is all of that going to fit inside me if I already feel so overwhelmed.

"Oh shit." I tremble, breaths speeding up. "Emmerich, I'm not sure—"

Klaus takes my chin and turns my head so I'm forced to look at him.

"Don't watch," he says. "Just feel."

I open my mouth to protest, but Emmerich chooses that moment to rock into me, and my body accepts him even though my brain is telling me it's impossible. He slides an inch deeper, the textured length of him doing crazy things to my insides.

"Okay." I grasp Klaus' horn and keep him anchored right in front of me. "I'll try."

Emmerich chuckles, though the sound is strained. "Distract her, Klaus."

"Mm." Klaus leans in and kisses me slowly, as if we have all the time in the world. "I can do that. But you have to close your eyes for me."

I hesitate for a second, then obey him. In the absence of my sight, I feel lost, so I grip the sheets on either side of me, clenching my hands into fists. But then I focus on my other senses. Emmerich's hands are on my hips, anchoring me beautifully. His cock pulls out of me, and Klaus tells him to stay still. I hear the click of a plastic cap and realize they're putting some of that lube on Emmerich's cock.

"Good idea," I croak, my eyes still shut. "Told you we'd need it."

"Hush."

Klaus's voice is closer now, and it's all the warning I get before his hot mouth closes around my left nipple and he sucks on the peak, hard. I arch into his touch, needing *more*, and Emmerich chooses that moment to sink back inside me.

"You're so gorgeous, Morgan." His voice is deeper than before. "Fuck, just wait until you feel the oil's effect. It's making my cock tingle."

I frown and nearly forget Klaus' order—because how can a tingling cock be a good thing? Then he pushes himself deeper, and the full sensation of the lube hits me.

It's not exactly *stimulating*—or an aphrodisiac—but it lets him glide better and lessens the friction. At the same time, it doesn't feel cold at all, like I'd expect lube to be. Instead, it's warm and tingly, like little pinpricks of light inside my pussy.

I let out a breathless giggle and pop my eyes open. "What the fuck? That feels amazing."

Klaus bites down lightly on my nipple. I jerk up, my surprised cry echoing around the room, but the pinch of pain is so damn good, I soften for Emmerich, allowing him to slide more of his length inside me.

"What did I say about looking?" Klaus admonishes me. "Now be good and close your eyes, Morgan."

I glare at him for a second, then obey, simply because I know he'll stop sucking my nipples if I don't. He rewards me with another careful bite, then puts his fingers to my clit and presses down, hard.

My entire body trembles from the onslaught of sensation. I've never been this full—or this stimulated. Together, they're hitting all the good points of my body, and I don't know how long I'll be able to hold off my orgasm. But I wanted to feel Emmerich come with me, so I grit my teeth and force myself to take several deep breaths through my nose.

"Oh, you're trying to hold back?"

Klaus' deep laugh caresses my senses. He nuzzles the valley between my breasts, his horns brushing against my skin. The sensation is new and strange at first—they're cool and raspy, the grooves and ridges gently scraping my skin, but the wicked gargoyle turns his head just so, and on his next move, the surface of the horn rubs right over my nipple.

I nearly levitate off the bed, then collapse underneath him, panting. All those deep breaths didn't work at all—I'm back to hovering at the edge of my orgasm, even though I've never come twice in one night before.

"That's it." Emmerich groans, and on the next slide, his

hips finally meet my ass, his cock sinking deep. "Yes, Morgan, yes!"

He feels incredible inside me. I can't help it—I open my eyes because I need to see this, I need the visual of Emmerich between my legs, of Klaus' evil grin as he plays my body exactly like I want him to.

"I'm going to come so deep inside you," Emmerich promises me. His words are coming faster, his accent deepening as he fights off his own climax. "Look at you. Fucking perfect." He lets out a string of German as if he's forgotten himself, then shakes his head sharply. "Klaus, I need to bite her."

With one last, quick lick, Klaus rears back, and for the first time since this began, I see how hard he is, his cock jutting up, leaking milky white precum onto the sheets beside me. He grasps the root of it and gives me a wink, and then all I can see is Emmerich, leaning down for a kiss.

I expected him to devour me, to fuck me hard and fast because this is our first time—and we can savor this later. But he slows right down and kisses me deeply, taking his time with me. Every roll of his hips sends sparks through me, a promise of a spectacular orgasm, his pubic bone nudging my clit with just enough pressure to spin me higher and higher.

"You are a dream," he murmurs against my ear. "You will come around my cock, and I will give you *all of me*, Morgan. I'm going to bite you, and then, when we're both spent and my seed is leaking out of you, Klaus will take you, too. He'll fuck all my cum back into your pussy, *Liebchen*."

My inner muscles contract at this, and I cry out, squeezing my eyes shut. Why the fuck is that so hot? I'm wearing the damn bracelet, so I *know* it's just talk—but maybe I won't be wearing it for as long as I thought.

"Yes," I whisper in his ear, my fingers digging into his thick black hair. "Do it, Emmerich."

He moves from my mouth to my neck, choosing the side opposite Klaus' bite. His fangs scrape my skin, and he hesitates for just a moment, as if he doesn't want to cause me pain.

So I grasp the back of his head and hold him close to me, letting him know I'm ready—more than ready, I *need* him to do this. To forge that connection between us, make it harder than iron, more durable than steel.

He withdraws his hips an inch, then two, making a sliver of space between us, then slams back inside, and at the same moment, sinks his teeth into my neck.

The pain radiates from the bite, but the way his cock fits inside me triggers my climax, shooting pleasure all through my body. Then I register the second source of bliss—the mating bond flaring to life, pulsing from the site of Emmerich's bite outward, a glow growing in my chest.

I open my mouth on a soundless scream and clench around Emmerich, clutching on with all I have—my inner muscles clamp around his length as if I could hold him inside me indefinitely. I wrap my legs around his waist and hook my ankles behind his back. He ruts mindlessly into me, then freezes, shouting his release. He releases my neck and arches up, so magnificent my heart threatens to pound its way out of my rib cage. I dig my fingernails into his shoulders and pull him down on top of me, not even caring that his weight could crush me.

He trembles above me, his hips twitching forward every few seconds, like he's shooting more hot cum into my pussy. I moan as his cock twitches inside me, but I don't let him go —I'm not sure I'll ever be able to.

I close my eyes, willingly this time, and focus on the second presence in my chest. It's Emmerich's essence, and I get to experience all the hope and love, all the awe he feels for me.

Tears well in my eyes and trickle down my temples and into my hair. I sniffle, then try to muffle the sound because I don't want to freak them out. But Emmerich lifts his head and grins at me—and I realize he feels my sensations mirrored inside him, too, so he knows I'm not crying because anything is wrong.

"I love you," he says, his expression softening. "So much."

I blink up at him, stunned. He said those words so casually, like they are meant to be said easily and often.

And maybe they are. Maybe this entire thing between the three of us can be easy, with no feelings held back, no reservations getting in the way.

"I love you, too," I blurt.

The confession feels so right on my tongue, I grin and say it again.

"I do." I laugh, more tears flowing. "I really do. And I love you, Klaus, even if you can't say it back yet."

Emmerich turns his head toward his first roost mate. "I love you, too. I always have and always will."

I have to stifle a sob at that because he's too sweet. Of course, he's still buried in my pussy, so maybe that's having an effect on him—but I just think Emmerich is like that, honest and pure and so damn loveable.

Klaus stares at us, his face a stony mask. I can't tell what he's thinking—whether he's shocked or scared or even angry, because he sure doesn't look happy. Then a pulse of pure joy erupts inside me, spreading through my veins, thrumming with the beat of my heart.

CHAPTER 20

MORGAN

I gasp, my hand flying to my chest.

It takes me a very confused moment to figure out it's *him*—it's the bond between Klaus and me, showing me exactly what he's experiencing. Emmerich's smile grows, and he simply leans forward, grasps Klaus by the back of his neck, and hauls him in for a kiss. Klaus goes willingly, almost as if he's too stunned to do anything but follow Emmerich's lead, which testifies to the depth of his surprise.

I think for a moment that he might not believe us, that he's trying to figure out whether we're both telling the truth, but if I can feel his emotions this strongly inside me, he must feel ours, too. He must know that I would never lie to him about this, and I wouldn't have said those words if they weren't true.

Emmerich finally releases him, and with a hiss, pulls out of my body. The obscene sound his cock makes as it slides free has me reaching down between my legs to cover my pussy because I can already feel the trickle of Emmerich's cum slipping out of me.

"Shit." I sit up to find a towel or something, but all that does is push more of the cum out, so I flop back on the pillows, flushing. "Um, guys, can you help me out?"

Emmerich stretches himself out on the blankets beside me and tucks his arms behind his head. His spent cock lies against his taut lower belly, trailing cum and my slickness all over his skin, but he doesn't seem to mind. He gives me a slow smile and says, "I won't wash tonight, *Liebchen*. I smell like you, and I want to stay that way for hours."

"Ohhh." My face must be burning, judging by how hot it feels. "But I'm *dripping*."

Klaus moves to lean over me. He takes my knees and spreads them. I resist a little, but he arches one eyebrow at me, and I loosen my muscles, allowing him to push my thighs apart.

Then he says, "Morgan…"

He's staring at my hand, which is still covering my pussy. I don't want to let go—don't want him to see the mess Emmerich and I created, but he taps my hand with one long finger and waits me out.

"If you could get me something to wipe myself…"

I only need a moment to compose myself, no more. Just a small pause to make sure I'm still sane enough to continue this, because I'm pretty sure Emmerich managed to rearrange the very molecules of my body.

Klaus reaches over the edge of the nest and brings up the shirt I wore earlier. He holds it just out of my reach, his expression severe. "I can give you this, and you'll be able to clean yourself. Or…" He makes a pause, running his gaze down my body and fixating on my hand again. "Or you can let me clean you up. Let me take care of you, Morgan."

I tremble under his focused stare. "Why?"

"Because I love you," he murmurs.

My tears well again. "You do?"

He offers me the shirt again, as if my question doesn't require an answer—and it doesn't. Because I can feel him, his emotions as clear as mine.

So instead of taking that shirt, I just shake my head…and remove my hand from between my legs.

Klaus drops the lump of fabric on the bed and focuses his gaze on my pussy. "So fucking *drenched*. You smell like Emmerich, *Engel*." He lowers himself until his broad shoulders are between my thighs, his wings folded tight against his back to keep from slamming into my legs. "My mouth is watering from the need to taste you."

I hike my knees higher, exposing myself to him. "I bet we taste amazing together."

It's something I never imagined I'd say, but it feels so right—and I want to tease Klaus a tiny bit more.

"But Emmerich promised me you'd fuck all his cum back inside me." I pout a little for show, my gaze connecting with his. "I don't know if I want—*oh*!"

He licks a long strip from my pussy to my clit, and I can't find any more words to poke fun at him. His groan is almost anguished, and when he grips my thighs to bring himself closer to me, his claws dig into my skin. He seems lost in me, slurping and sliding around, eating up everything. My tired body is slow to respond at first, but he's relentless, winding the need in me higher and higher until I'm rocking my hips up, chasing more contact.

Then he suddenly surges up, his cock hard against my belly. He kisses me on the mouth, and I get to taste him—combined with Emmerich's cum and my juices, and it's the single most erotic thing I've ever experienced.

He sucks on my tongue, then moves over to press kisses

to my jaw, right up to my temple, where he licks away my tears.

"Salty," he murmurs, then licks again. "I've never tasted human tears before, Morgan. I can't get enough."

I whimper because I was so close to my climax before, but he takes his time, kissing and licking me. I return every caress and tug on his horns to keep him where I want him, because I need him to know that this is just as special as what I did with Emmerich—I don't want to rush a moment of this.

Emmerich doesn't interfere for once, like he senses the sharpness of Klaus' need and wants him to have me all for himself. His essence pulses through me, contentment radiating from him in waves. Then I realize he's enjoying what Klaus is doing to me—because he feels every single thing, too.

It's wild, this connection between the three of us, and I can't wait to explore it more.

But when I reach down to wrap my palm around Klaus' cock, he growls, his hips bucking into my grip.

"Wicked human," he snarls. "Making me lose control."

I barely touched him—so I know he must be riding the edge. I want to come, yes, but more than that, I want to make him feel so good.

I grasp him tighter and run my hand from his root to the broad tip, then down again—and I suddenly find myself airborne.

Klaus lunges for me so fast, I don't register he's moving me until I'm face down on the pillows, my ass in the air.

He shifts behind me, both hands on my cheeks, and spreads me rudely. My face flushes at the thought of how I must look, so exposed and indecent.

But Klaus doesn't let me think too much about it. Something warm and supple glides into my pussy, and I gasp, realizing it's his tail. He spreads me out slowly while he reaches under my body to press his fingers to my clit.

"Are you ready to take me, Morgan?" he murmurs, his lips hot on my shoulder. "I need to be inside you and I'll take you hard and fast."

"I'm ready," I promise him. "Don't hold back."

His tail slips away from me, but before I can protest the loss of sensation, Klaus notches his cockhead at my pussy lips and pushes forward, the movement assured and steady. My mouth falls open on a gasp as I try to keep myself relaxed and soft for him. I know I can take him—he can't be that much larger than Emmerich—but it's like we're doing this again for the first time and my body has to relearn how to accept an intrusion this big.

"You look so perfect, so good."

Klaus' rumbling praise is something I never knew I needed, but now I crave it more with every minute—his reassurance that we'll get through this. Because I'm just not sure…

Then he brushes aside the mess of my hair and clamps his big hand around the back of my neck, squeezing lightly. "You're clenching around me too hard."

I close my eyes, a whimper escaping my lips. I *love* the pressure of his hand, but it's sending me closer to my orgasm, which means that yes, I'm clenching around him. "I can't help it."

He hums, his thumb caressing the side of my neck, right over my pulse point. It's dangerous, having his claws right there, but *fuck*, it feels good. I push myself back, wanting to impale myself deeper, but all that does is strain our connection, and I stop, whimpering.

"Emmerich, we need your help."

Klaus motions with his other hand, and Emmerich scoots

over immediately. He's hard again, his cock bobbing, but he only has eyes for me.

"What should I do?" He palms my face gently, his expression so sincere. "Should I tease your pretty tits, *Liebchen*? Or your clit? I can hold your hand if you need me to."

I shake my head—my issue isn't that I can't get off but that I'm thinking too hard, trying with all I have to get myself to relax, which is having the opposite effect. So I have to focus on something else, something that will take my mind off Klaus' monster cock trying to push deep into my pussy.

"Sit right here." I pat the pillows in front of me. "And spread your legs."

Emmerich sends Klaus a shocked look, his eyebrows raised.

But our third roost mate just chuckles, the sound darker than before. "You heard the lady."

Emmerich scrambles to obey and settles against the pillows, his thick thighs wide, his cock now inches from my face. I glance up at him to see if he's okay with this and find him smiling down at me.

He palms my cheek again and tips my chin up. "We'll take care of you, and you'll take care of us. That's how things are done in the roost, you see?"

I nod, understanding flashing through me. "We need this, don't we?" I glance over my shoulder to find Klaus watching me with barely leashed passion and add, "It had to be all three of us, together."

I was worried over how we'd do this threesome thing. If one of us would always feel excluded. But if we can all do this together…

He nods, his beautiful mouth curling up in a wry smile. "It was always going to end this way."

A sense of peace settles over me, and I relax underneath him even before I grasp the root of Emmerich's magnificent cock and lean forward to take it in my mouth. The moment my inner muscles soften, Klaus pushes forward, his cock sliding more easily inside me. He pauses for a moment to add more of the spelled lube, and it works perfectly, warming my slightly sore tissue, making it easier for him to thrust deeper.

"Fuck, you feel good." Klaus' words are turning unintelligible, his growls louder and louder. "I never dreamed—I always wished—"

He seems to be at a loss for words, so I reach back with my other hand to touch his knee where he has it braced on the bed next to me. At the same time, I take Emmerich's cock deep, so deep the tip of him brushes the back of my throat, and I have to pull back for a bit. He lets out a low moan and tangles his fingers in my hair, massaging my scalp and showing me just how fast he needs me to suck him.

When Klaus bottoms out, his hips flush with my ass, I moan around Emmerich's cock, my body trembling already. I was close before, and now, with every one of Klaus' strokes gliding so perfectly over my G-spot, I'm holding back with all I have.

But Klaus knows exactly what I'm doing. "Let go," he orders, his palm landing between my shoulder blades, a possessive touch I crave. "I need you to come, Morgan. I need to feel your pussy strangling my cock so I can give you all my cum."

I whimper and close my eyes. He pounds into me, and each thrust moves me forward, so I give up trying to keep a steady rhythm of sucking Emmerich's cock. Instead, I give myself over completely to them and let all their praise, all their groans of pleasure sink into me, permeate through my skin and soak my soul until I don't know where I end and they begin.

My orgasm starts as a small starburst in my belly, and I resist it for a moment longer, whimpering around

Emmerich's cock. It thickens impossibly, the ridges gliding over my tongue, the precum dripping in a steady stream, and he wraps his hand in my hair and tugs lightly as if he's warning me, trying to tell me he's close to coming.

But I want *all* of him, so I sink deeper on my next suck, so low his cockhead bumps the back of my throat. Then I hold it there and attempt something I never have before—and swallow.

Emmerich's big body goes taut, and he grips me harder, his claws digging into my scalp. My eyelids flutter at the pinch of pain, my body hovering on the edge of the precipice.

Klaus chooses that moment to press down on my clit and buries his whole length inside me. My mind blanks, and then I'm coming—the pleasure is so strong, my vision tunnels, and all my muscles seize up, including my hand around Emmerich's shaft.

His shout of pleasure echoes around the room, and his cum shoots onto my tongue, straight into my throat. I swallow all I can, then gasp as Klaus fucks me harder, each thrust hitting my G-spot so well, pinpricks of light dance in my vision, my climax going on and on, prolonged by theirs.

The next rush of Emmerich's cum lands on my chin and chest, hot and fragrant. I'm trembling all over, almost too stimulated, when Klaus snarls, his body curling over mine. He covers me completely and stops thrusting, holding himself so deep inside me as he empties himself in my pussy.

I feel the jets of his cum like fresh thrusts inside me, and I regret—for the briefest of moments—the bracelet I'm wearing.

I brush the thought aside for now. It's too soon to be thinking about that, but I know deep in my heart that we'll be having that conversation soon. Perhaps sooner than Emmerich and Klaus think.

It takes me long minutes to catch my breath, and my

gargoyles aren't faring any better. Klaus pulls out of me almost reluctantly and rolls to lie beside us while Emmerich draws me into his lap and stares down between my legs, where Klaus' cum is now trickling slowly from my pussy.

"God, I'm a mess." I push back my hair and reach for the shirt Klaus discarded earlier. "I think I need a quick wash."

Emmerich freezes, his arms tightening around me. "You-you want to wash?"

I glance up at him. "That's what humans usually do after sex, yeah."

His jaw works, the muscles in his cheek twitching. Then he blurts out, "Do you think you could wait just a little?"

I can't help it—something in my chest melts at his urgency. "Is this a scent thing? Do you like me smelling like you?"

He nods, looking more than a little embarrassed. "I'm sorry."

"Don't be." I turn to Klaus, finding him watching us intently. "I'll give it a couple of hours, okay? Then I'll have to wash, or I'll get all crusty and nasty."

Emmerich's grin is wide enough to show off his fangs. "Deal."

Klaus reaches out, takes my hand, and presses a kiss to the inside of my palm. "I am undone every time you accept something so easily, *Engel*. Every time you don't run away when we say something like this."

I wrap my fingers around his horn and give it a light tug. "Well, it's the least I can do, especially after you both went out of your way to make this Christmas the best I've ever had."

At that, both gargoyles jerk to attention, their sleepy, easy demeanor gone.

"What?" I ask. "What did I say?"

Klaus jumps to his feet and drags on his pants, his wings high with agitation.

Emmerich takes me by my waist and deposits me gently on the pillows. "We forgot to feed you," he growls. "It's been *hours*. Don't worry, Morgan, we'll take care of you now."

"But I don't—" I begin, then stop when I notice the determined glint of his eyes.

Whatever instinct is driving them, I guess I'll have to accept that, too.

"Rest, Morgan," Klaus commands. "And no peeking."

Feeling very loved, I flop back and throw my arm over my eyes to show them how seriously I'm following their orders. "I'll stay right here, don't worry."

CHAPTER 21

MORGAN

I wake up with a start, the scent of cooking meat in my nostrils. I could swear I was dreaming about something beautiful, but the images slip away before I can remember.

Then I blink and realize it wasn't a dream at all—I really am in an old stone tower, still naked in the nest that my gargoyle mates built for me.

One of them must have covered me to keep me from getting chilled because I'm cozy under a fluffy wool blanket. My heart leaps happily at the thought—they're so incredibly thoughtful and mindful of my human needs.

Speaking of which—I really have to go pee.

Wrapping myself in the blanket, I scoot to the edge of the nest and get to my feet, slightly wobbly from all my physical exertions and sleep. My movement must catch the gargoyles' eyes because they both turn toward me from where they're crouched by the fireplace, their wings hiding the flames from view.

"I'm just going to the bathroom," I explain, already walking toward the door.

But Klaus is by my side immediately and scoops me up into his arms. "Your feet will get chilled on the stairway," he rumbles by way of explanation. "If you need to go out there, let us know."

I narrow my eyes at him but don't protest—for now. Eventually, we'll have to find a way for me to go to the toilet unassisted. I'm thinking fur-lined boots or maybe some really thick wool slippers, the kind that go up to the ankle?

I think I'll enjoy making this place my home.

My heart skips a beat as I consider this. We haven't exactly talked about me moving in, but I can't imagine going back to my drab apartment for any length of time. Not when my gargoyles are *here*.

The thought occupies me while Klaus carries me downstairs and I do my business in the bathroom. I do clean myself up just slightly, using a warm, damp hand towel, and also rake my fingers through my messy curls, attempting to tame them.

Klaus raises one eyebrow at me as if he can sense the newfound unease squirming in my belly but doesn't push me—and I love him a little more for it. We have enough time to talk about this, surely, and I don't have to dump this issue on them right now.

But the moment I see Emmerich at the fireplace, looking so cozy and happy to see us, something in my belly squeezes painfully, and I can't hold back.

"Can I move in with you?" I blurt, my voice coming out all croaky and weird. "I mean, I thought…I thought that maybe you'd want me to stay."

"Yes, of course," Emmerich says, flicking his hand as if that's a done deal in his mind. "Now come here, the steaks are done."

I swallow, my throat tight with emotion. He-he just *accepts* this? Without even discussing it?

A glance up at Klaus tells me he's aware of my shock. He sets me gently on the floor, then takes my chin in his big hand and presses a slow kiss to my lips. "Would you like to move in with us, Morgan? We'll have to build a front door on the bottom floor to be able to give you the keys to our tower, so you might have to wait a while, but that's a formality." He slides his hand to the back of my neck, squeezing. "We want you here."

Emmerich glances up, then seems to realize that this is a bigger issue than he thought. He stands and comes to hug me from behind. "I'm sorry, *Liebchen*, I thought you understood how much we need you here. I want to wake up next to you every morning and fuck you every night. Hard to do without you living here."

I let out a laugh and lean back in his arms, my knees suddenly weak. "All right. Yes, I'll move in with you. Thank you."

"We can go get your things when the weather clears up," Klaus says. "Until then, I'm afraid you're trapped in the tower with us."

Heat surges through me at his suggestive words. "Oh, no." I clutch at my chest, which is still covered with nothing but a blanket. "However will I cope?"

He grins, then smacks my ass playfully. "All right, enough chatting. Emmerich is right, the steaks are done, and they're getting cold."

We take the seats in front of the fireplace, and Emmerich serves me a most curious Christmas dinner.

"We looked up human food on the internet," he explains as he uses the poker to dig a slightly charred potato from the embers, then picks it up and drops it on my plate. "There are more potatoes if you'd like, and we warmed up the green beans like the tin said."

I wince as he grabs the tin from the fire without so much as yelping in pain. "This is wonderful, but, ah, I'll need your help opening it. I'm not as flame retardant as you seem to be."

This results in lots of cursing and a search for a hunting knife, which Klaus swears he put back in the drawer after last using it, but is finally found in his coat pocket. When we're settled back at the fireplace, me with my potato and beans, them with still-empty plates, Emmerich takes a giant cast-iron pan from the embers. On it are several enormous steaks, some of which look almost entirely raw.

I eye the meat with trepidation—will they be insulted if I ask for my meat to be well done?

But Emmerich grins at me, his expression smug. "Do not worry, Morgan. I read that most humans like their meat cooked, so I put yours on first." He points to two massive slabs of meat that have some nice browning on them. "Klaus said I was ruining your meal, but I don't think I did that, did I?"

"Nope, you did well." I breathe a sigh of relief and offer him my plate. "But, uh, let's just start with *one* of those."

Klaus shakes his head in disbelief. "Maybe I will get you to see the error of your ways."

I squint at his steak, which is still dripping blood. "I don't think so. I won't ask you to eat my meat if you don't make me eat yours."

His gray eyes light up with humor. "All right, human, you have a deal."

It's the strangest Christmas meal I've ever experienced, but it's exactly how it's supposed to be. Cozy and filled with laughter, a little weird but delicious.

"Guys?" My voice catches on the word, so I set down my

plate, clear my throat, and try again. "I-I'm really glad you found me in the woods."

Klaus reaches out and entwines his fingers with mine. "And I'm glad you went searching for us in the first place."

Emmerich nods, his left wing opening to hug me around my shoulders. "You knew exactly where to find us."

My heart thumps happily at their words. I press my lips together to hide a smile and say, "You *do* realize I was searching for bats, yes?"

Klaus' admonishing glare has me squirming in my seat, and I know I'll pay for my cheek—not that I mind at all. He sets his empty plate aside and stands, looming over me. Emmerich's grinning at us already, his hands on his knees as if he's just waiting to leap into action.

"You're way better than bats, though," I backtrack, craning my neck to stare at Klaus.

He moves so fast, I can barely track his movements, and a second later, I'm hanging upside down over his shoulder, my blanket slipping to the floor.

"Emmerich, save me!" I giggle and kick my feet, which has no effect whatsoever on Klaus.

He slaps my ass, the smack reverberating around the room, then tosses me in the middle of our nest, where I land in a pile of pillows.

Emmerich is there, already undoing his pants. "Oh, no, human, there's no saving you now."

I expect Klaus to pin me down and fuck me fast, but instead, he throws himself down right next to me and pulls me on top of him so my back is flush with his front. He spreads my legs wide, exposing me to Emmerich, and I gasp when I realize his intention.

"This is what you get for teasing us," he rumbles in my ear, then licks a stripe over my neck, right where his mating bite is. "You'll learn that we'll always reward you for it."

I melt at his words, and when Emmerich kneels between our legs and brings his mouth to my pussy, I'm ready for him. He licks my clit with surgical precision, listening to my every cue, and in minutes, I'm a panting, writhing mess. It must be the mating bond—and the fact that all my hot spots are still sensitive from our earlier round of sex.

When I'm dripping all over Klaus, they work together to lift me and settle me onto his cock. It slides deep without issue this time—I'm too turned on to worry about this anymore. Klaus pumps his hips up, and I realize I have no leverage to push back, apart from squeezing my inner muscles around him. He brings both hands to my tits and pinches my nipples just how I like it, hard enough to hurt.

My moan is indecent, and it fuels their lust as much as mine. Klaus thrusts faster, his ridged cock dragging over my G-spot with every push, and Emmerich fists his erection, stroking it in time with our movements. Neither of them speaks, as if they're too far gone for it. I have no words either—there's only the slip and slide and our panting breaths, the perfect soundtrack to this moment.

Then Emmerich leans over and puts his mouth back to my clit, his hot, rough tongue scraping over my enlarged bud with such perfect pleasure, I scream in surprise, my eyes flying open.

I wasn't even aware I'd closed them—but now I fight to keep them open because I'm afraid I'll lose myself in the sensations if I don't.

Klaus bites down on my earlobe, his teeth sharp against my skin, and murmurs, "I feel your pussy trying to suck all my cum from me. Come for us, and I'll give you everything I have."

I tremble, feeling unmoored—this is too intense, and I can't see either of them well. Emmerich is busy between my legs, and Klaus is right behind me. I don't want to move from this position because it's so damn good, but…

Klaus moves one hand from my breast to my neck, his long fingers closing around it. He puts his lips to my ear and rasps, "I'm right here, Morgan. *We're* right here with you, and you're safe. Come for us, now. Be good and give us—*ah!*"

He groans as my body tightens, and my entire being shrinks down to the perfect pleasure of having Klaus inside me and Emmerich licking my clit.

I clutch Klaus' arm as I come, clinging on to him. He feels so damn solid, so *real*, and I don't ever want to let go. Emmerich licks up every drop of my pleasure, then straightens and stares down at me, his fist flying over his cock. Klaus groans and snaps his hips up faster, and within moments, he's spilling himself inside me, his grip on me tightening, as if he, too, needs me to ground him. Emmerich throws his head back in pleasure and squeezes his cock hard. His cum splashes all over my belly and thighs, coating my pussy and the base of Klaus' cock as he groans and shudders between our legs.

When he finally pries his eyes open again, he gives us the most devastatingly handsome grin and leans forward to kiss me, then Klaus, not caring one bit that he's now also covered in his own cum.

"*Now* our Christmas really is perfect," he purrs, satisfaction radiating down our mating bond. "I will have to see if there are more human holidays we can celebrate with such excellent results."

I giggle at the idea of what other humans would think of such celebrations. "Well, there's Easter in April and…Fourth of July, I guess? And Thanksgiving, of course. If we want to stretch it a little, we can also count Memorial Day and Labor Day and…"

Klaus hugs me close to his chest, his thick arms like iron bands around my belly. "We can do this *every* day if we want."

Emmerich blinks, then nods vehemently. "Yes, why not. Every day with my mates is like a holiday."

My eyes well with tears at his sweet words. With them, I don't have to wonder what my future will bring because I know already that it will be filled with love. And probably lots of sex. And to me, that beats anything else I could think of.

"I agree. Let's do this every day."

EPILOGUE

MORGAN

Six months later

I hold on to Klaus, my body soft and pliant after the fantastic orgasm he just gave me.

"I knew it," I grumble as he carries me up the stairs to the roof. "You had an ulterior motive when you did that thing with your tail."

He grins down at me, unrepentant. "Emmerich and I agreed it would make flying easier for you if you were more relaxed."

"Humans weren't made for flying." My heart rate is already picking up at the thought of being carried around in that harness. "I'm really sorry, but I still prefer to have both my feet firmly on the ground."

Klaus hums, then nudges open the door to the rooftop

terrace. "You agreed to try again," he reminds me gently. "But if you hate it *that* much, we can always do something else instead."

I think about quitting for a moment. Then I notice Emmerich standing at the edge of the landing platform, the tandem harness already strapped to his chest. He's bouncing on the balls of his feet, excitement radiating from him, and I realize I couldn't possibly refuse him now.

"No, that's fine," I murmur to Klaus. "I'll live. And maybe I'll get used to it someday."

He kisses my forehead and sets me on my feet. "Good. Remember, you don't have to trust that human harness. Emmerich would never let you fall."

"I know." I return Klaus' kiss, standing on tiptoes, then pat his naked chest and walk over to Emmerich.

Our roost mate swoops me up in a hug and twirls me around, sending my summer dress fluttering. "Ah, did you see what a beautiful Friday evening it is?" He stops and turns me toward the west, where the last vestiges of the sunset have painted the sky a deep, gorgeous purple. "And look, the stars have come out. It's a perfect night for flying, *Liebchen*."

I grin up at him. His enthusiasm is contagious, as always. He loves flying so much, I make an effort to let him take me up at least once a week. Sometimes, Klaus does it, too. He claims that I just need to get desensitized, and perhaps he's correct. I'm not dreading this flight as much as usual. The nice weather—a warm evening with no wind to speak of—is helping, of course. I know firsthand that flying in windy, rainy conditions is *not* pleasant for humans, even though gargoyles enjoy it immensely.

"Help us get strapped in?" I throw a glance over my shoulder at Klaus. "I can't reach the buckles at my back."

He steps in and guides me to put my arms through the correct loops. We'd modified the harness slightly to allow me to be turned *toward* Emmerich rather than away, because flying with my back to his chest was even more terrifying. I'd figured out early on that I didn't enjoy dangling over nothingness, even if the view was better. If I faced Emmerich's chest, I could bury my face in his neck whenever I got too scared, and I could hold on to his shoulders for added support.

He didn't even mind if I dug my fingernails in his leathery skin. There were definitely some perks to having an inhuman boyfriend.

Klaus kisses my bare shoulder. "You're all set." He leans in and brushes his lips over Emmerich's, too. "Do you want me out there with you?"

Emmerich tugs him in, so I'm suddenly caught in a gargoyle sandwich—my favorite place to be.

"You shouldn't miss an evening this fine," he tells Klaus. "We could fly east, over the forest. There's nothing out there for miles if we keep away from the roads."

Klaus' smile is a thing of beauty. "All right. Lead the way."

I grip the back of Emmerich's neck, tensing in anticipation of the launch.

He wraps one arm around me, squeezing me to his chest, then leaps off the roof. His massive wings snap open and catch the wind, carrying us up and away from the tower, over the dark forest. My belly swoops with each dip and turn, and I let out a squeak of terror as he banks sharply—but he's only circling around Klaus who has joined us now. His silhouette is barely visible to me, an inky blot in the indigo night sky.

Emmerich takes the lead and carries me away from Clearwater, far from the town lights. We're high enough that I barely dare to look down, but there in the distance, a car drives through the night, its red taillights disappearing into the darkness.

I relax marginally with each passing minute, and after a while, I glance up instead.

A canopy of stars lights our way, brilliant pinpricks of light scattered across the sky. The moon hasn't risen yet, and for once, I'm glad, even if it means I can't see Emmerich and Klaus as clearly. This far from any big city, light pollution fades away, and the darker it gets, the more stars are visible above us.

Emmerich murmurs the names of the constellations to me, then points out Jupiter, one of the brightest dots in the sky.

"It's beautiful," I tell him. "Thank you for bringing me up here."

He nuzzles my cheek then adjusts his wings slightly to dive right, in Klaus' direction. "You hear that? Morgan is *happy* to be here!"

Klaus whistles in encouragement, and I grin, knowing he can see my expression.

"Fine, fine," I call out, "I'll admit it, your plan worked! I *am* more relaxed tonight."

Emmerich puts his nose to my temple and inhales deeply. "*Ja*, and you smell so good, too. I want to fuck you the moment we return."

His words rekindle the need that Klaus sated only partially before. He'd licked my pussy, bringing me to a very fast, very satisfying orgasm, but he hasn't fucked me yet today—which I suspect was on purpose as well. He'd wanted me to remain on edge, at least a little distracted before the flight.

I close my eyes and mirror Emmerich's gesture, inhaling his clean scent. My need grows stronger, my body begging for more, as it always does in my mates' presence.

"Mm." Emmerich palms my ass with both hands,

kneading my flesh through the fabric of my dress. "What are you thinking of, Morgan?"

Squirming in his grip, I pull myself higher up his body, straining the reach of the harness, and put my legs around his waist. "I think…"

"Yes?" he prompts, his palms now on my naked thighs. "Tell me what you need."

"I want you inside me," I admit. "Can we try?"

Emmerich's wings snap out as he hovers in place, waiting for Klaus to circle around. "Right now? You want me to fuck you right now?"

Klaus sweeps past us, a whiff of his scent sending my need spiraling even higher. I grasp Emmerich's long hair and wind it around my fist, then tug lightly. He lets out an indecent moan, and his cock hardens between us, straining against his leather pants.

"No, *I* want to fuck you," I murmur, licking his neck. The taste of his skin has me closing my eyes in pleasure. "And I need you to keep us in the air."

We haven't done this yet—and maybe it's madness. I sure as hell wouldn't have attempted it when we first started flying in the winter. The first time Emmerich took me out for a short moonlit flight, I'd clutched on to his jacket and kept my eyes shut the entire time, much to his chagrin.

But right now, with Klaus flying around us to offer help if needed, and with desire for *both* thrumming through my veins…

"Yes," Emmerich says. "I will keep us in the air. But I'm turning back toward the tower now so I can fuck you, too."

Klaus' deep laughter floats to us on a breeze. "This is madness, but if it works, it might just be my new favorite thing to do."

I grin at him, my belly tightening with need. Yeah, if we survive this without any bumps and bruises, I'll fly with him next time. But right now, I need to figure out how to do this…

Emmerich squeezes my thighs, then runs his palms under my skirt to my panties. With a quick tug of his sharp claws, he shreds the cotton and wads up my underwear in his fist, then lets out a shrill whistle to alert Klaus. The next moment, my panties flutter through the air, and Klaus snatches them up, brings them to his nose and inhales deeply.

"Fuck, Morgan, you're *drenched*," he growls, his next pass bringing him closer to us. "I thought I licked you clean earlier, but you're giving Emmerich more, aren't you?"

Emmerich's fingers move between my legs. He's always so careful with his claws, but he runs a knuckle over my slick pussy lips and groans. "She's ready for me, Klaus."

I love it how they take control—but this little experiment was *my* idea. Reaching between our bodies, I undo the buttons at the fly of Emmerich's pants and shove the fabric apart, freeing his erection. He's hard already, the long, thick cock weeping at the tip. I grasp it tightly in my fist and run my palm down its ridged length, relishing the way Emmerich's wings twitch at my touch.

"Better gain some altitude," he murmurs, spiraling up on a current of air. "So we have more space to work with."

I guide the broad cockhead to my pussy, hoisting myself up a fraction higher to line myself up. "Steady, now."

The head slips inside me, and we both groan at the stretching sensation. If Klaus hadn't made me come earlier, this would have been an even tighter fit, but I'm still loose and soft from that orgasm.

With Emmerich's hands on my ass, I roll my hips and work myself onto Emmerich's length, taking a half inch at a time.

"God, how does this *always* feel so good?"

I moan as the tip of his cock nudges my G-spot, then

push myself away from his chest for leverage. On the next exhale, I let myself sink farther onto him. The way we fit together has all my senses firing up. My nipples tighten under my bra, and I clench my inner muscles around Emmerich, drawing a guttural groan from him.

"The sounds you're making..."

Klaus' growl sounds close, so I look over my shoulder to find him flying in tandem with us, the tip of his right wing nearly brushing Emmerich's left. He's too far for me to reach out, but it feels like he's *with* us, his scorching gaze burning my skin.

It prompts me to do what I've been thinking of for months.

I lock my hands around Emmerich's neck and fumble with the bracelet that was his Christmas present to me. It's been such a help, allowing us to get to know each other before expanding our family.

I've made good friends with Irma, our supplier of witchy goods—such as the magic lube, which we buy so often, I'd be embarrassed about it if Irma didn't have such a down-to-earth attitude toward sex. We've been visiting her every month just before the full moon to replenish the contraceptive charm on the bracelet, but if it all goes well, we won't need to for a while.

The dainty clasp of the bracelet slips free, and I barely catch the chain before it tumbles into the darkness below. I grasp it in my fist, then search for where Klaus is flying next to us. Taking a cue from Emmerich's earlier stunt with my panties, I whistle. It sounds much less cool than Emmerich's shrill signal, but Klaus still turns his head toward me.

I toss him the bracelet, hoping I didn't misjudge his night vision and dexterity. I shouldn't have worried. He snatches it from the air easily and stares at it, hovering in midair.

"What was that?" Emmerich asks. "Morgan, what did you do?"

I grin, but before I can answer, Klaus lets out a rumbling purr.

"Her bracelet," he replies. "She took it off."

Emmerich is silent for a shocked beat, then lowers his forehead to mine. "You're certain?"

I nod, holding on tight to his shoulders. "I want this."

To punctuate my words, I raise my knees slightly, getting a better angle between our bodies. Emmerich's cock sinks all the way inside me, hitting all the right places. He lets out an inhuman sound, a growl so deep, I feel it all through my body, a vibration that has me squirming even as I roll my hips for more.

"This feels incredible," I gasp, rocking myself on his hardness. "Emmerich, I'm not going to last."

I glance up when he doesn't answer—and realize he's gritting his teeth, his expression determined. I didn't even notice, but he's focused on flying, his wings working hard to carry us back home.

"Hey." I move one palm to his cheek and caress his leathery skin. "Are you okay?"

He smiles down at me, but it's different than before, almost feral in its intensity. "Oh, yes, *Liebchen*. I only want a wall to push you up against so I can fuck my cum so deep inside you, it will make a baby tonight."

My inner muscles clench at his crude words, and I gasp, my climax hovering close. "It won't—it's not the right time of the month." I moan as he squeezes my ass and pulls me closer, impaling me on his cock. "I only just finished with my period."

The gargoyles have been remarkably blase about my periods so far. They've read all about it, so now Klaus draws me a bath every time I've got cramps, gets into the clawfoot tub with me, and strokes my clit until I come because apparently, orgasms are the best pain relief.

But Emmerich is already shaking his head. "I don't care. I'll be inside you every day until you're carrying our young."

Klaus is completely silent—he hasn't uttered a word since he caught the bracelet. I try to meet his gaze, but he's flying just behind us, and Emmerich's wings are obscuring my view of him.

I hope he's okay with this.

We've talked about having children, and I've studied gargoyles and the possible outcomes of a relationship such as ours. When I confided my worries in Irma and Arielle, they informed me that Clearwater has a school for supernatural kids, one that accommodates all the individual species' needs —including a salt-water pool for baby aquatic creatures such as kraken and merpeople. Turns out, gargoyles aren't even the most complex of the supernaturals out there.

A dark shape materializes in the forest beneath us, and I realize we've returned home—it's our tower, its windows shuttered so no light filters through, just in case any other curious explorers are wandering in the woods, searching for the source of the local scary stories.

Now that I've come to live full-time at the tower, we've actually asked Irma and her friends to put up a protective spell for us, one that discourages most humans from coming anywhere close to our home.

Right now, I'm grateful for it because I'm flying without underwear, impaled on my gargoyle mate's cock, minutes from what I know will be a spectacular orgasm.

"Hold on," Emmerich orders just before he dives for the landing platform. "I've got you."

He lands neatly, but the movement still bounces me on his cock, and I cry out, the pleasure almost too intense.

Then Klaus is there, plastering himself against my back.

"I'll help," he growls, his hungry lips at my neck. "Fuck her, Emmerich. Give her all your cum so I can fuck it deep inside her when I replace you."

Emmerich kisses me fiercely, unrestrained now that we're on firm ground. The harness is both a help and a hindrance —it holds me in place, allowing Emmerich to touch me freely, but at the same time, I'm pinned to him, without much leverage to move now that they're both working together.

"You're a fucking *dream*," Klaus rasps in my ear. "I want to take your ass, Morgan, but I won't. Not until you're with our child. Not a drop of my cum will go to waste."

I gasp as Emmerich's cockhead hits my G-spot over and over, sending sparks of pleasure through my nerve endings. "Oh, fuck! I'm so close."

"I feel your tight pussy clenching around my cock," Emmerich growls. "You're hungry for my cum, aren't you? You'll milk it all from me?"

"Yes!" I don't know why this filthy talk of breeding and cum is doing it for me, but it *is*, and I'm barreling toward my orgasm, a runaway train with no stop in sight. "I want this so much. Please, Emmerich, please!"

He snarls, then picks up the pace, his hips snapping against mine in a brutal rhythm. If I was pressed up against a wall, I'd be bruised all over, but it's Klaus who's standing behind me, anchoring us in place, and he holds me so carefully, his hands firm on my hips, his broad chest bracketing my shoulders.

"Do you need me to pinch your clit?" he rumbles, his teeth grazing my earlobe. "Or will you come on Emmerich's dick without it, *Engel*? Is his thick cock enough to send you over?"

I whimper, colorful spots dancing behind my eyelids as I scrunch my eyes shut. "It's enough—it's always eno-*oh!*"

My climax hits me hard, blanking out my senses. Fireworks

explode in my belly, and I clench around Emmerich's cock, milking him just as he asked. He buries his thick length deep and comes with me, and I shudder in his arms, gasping for breath.

"Fuck!" He ruts inside me, hot jets of his cum heating my inner walls. "Morgan!"

The harness is a good accessory, I decide as my body grows limp from pleasure, my muscles relaxing completely. "Mm."

Emmerich's chest heaves like a bellows, and he's running his palms all over my back, my ass, my legs, as if he can't get enough of me. He nuzzles my cheek, then grins at Klaus over my shoulder. "That was a lot of cum."

I wince, already feeling it drip from my pussy, even though Emmerich is still hard inside me. "Yeah, you made a mess. But I love it."

"Careful, now," Klaus says. "Pull out slowly, and I'll slide right in."

I half twist in Emmerich's arms. "What? We're not going downstairs? I could at least wash…"

But Emmerich is already shaking his head. "*Nein, Liebchen*. You must stay with us all the time now. We will nest together, yes, but Klaus needs you."

"I have work on Monday," I remind them. "You'll have to let me go eventually."

Klaus rakes his teeth over my pulse point, sending shivers down my spine. "Mm, if you insist. That means we have more than forty-eight hours to be with you, though."

I grip Emmerich's shoulder more tightly, concern flaring through me. "By this, do you mean…?"

"We'll be inside you all this time, Morgan." Klaus moves his hands to my ass and shifts me a fraction, allowing Emmerich to slide almost all the way out. "If I'm not buried balls-deep in your pussy, Emmerich will be."

Emmerich kisses me on the lips, his tongue slicking over my bottom lip. "Don't worry, we will take good care of you. We have Irma's lotion for you if you get sore."

"Guys…" I gasp as Emmerich's thick cockhead teases my opening—not quite deep enough, yet still plugging the majority of the cum. "I'll need rest. And food. You know—"

"We know how to take care of our mate," Klaus rumbles, his voice fierce. "Do you trust us, Morgan?"

That's a question I can answer without hesitation. "Yes!"

"Then trust me with this." He glances at Emmerich, then adds, "Ready?"

At Emmerich's nod, Klaus lifts me from his mate's cock, then slides his own in place. With how wet and pliant I am, Klaus sinks deep in one long, delicious thrust. He molds his body to mine, protecting me. He moves his hands from my waist to Emmerich's and pulls us all closer together until I'm squished between them. I can't move—I can only take what Klaus decides to give me.

"I can't go slow," he growls into my neck, holding himself deep inside me. "I can't be gentle."

"Good." I reach down to cover his hand and intertwine my fingers with his. "I don't want that tonight."

With a snarl, he rocks his hips up, impaling me fully on his length. The ridged length of his erection drags over my sensitive G-spot as he pulls almost all the way out, then slams himself back in. He sets a punishing rhythm, and I love it—it feels as if he picked up right where Emmerich left me, right on the tail end of my climax, and he pushes me higher still.

Emmerich is the one anchoring us now, his hands moving over my skin, touching Klaus, teasing us both. He kisses me nice and slow, a delicious counterpoint to Klaus' increasingly brutal thrusts. I close my eyes and let myself ride the wave of pleasure building inside me, the spectacular orgasm looming ever closer.

"I love you," Klaus growls against my skin. "I love you both so much. I can't—" He rocks inside me again, his words broken, his voice almost desperate.

I reach back and grasp one of his horns, holding him as close to me as I can. "I love you, too. I'm so glad you found me."

Emmerich kisses me again, his hand on my cheek so tender. "You are my world." Then he looks at Klaus, his expression open and full of love. "And I'm so lucky I get to spend the rest of my life with you."

Klaus cries out, his back bowing from the force of his pleasure. He buries himself so deep, I know I'll feel him for days, then shoves his hand into the tight space between my body and Emmerich's. "Come for me, Morgan. Come for me, and I'll give you all my cum."

I'm so attuned to him, so close to the edge, I cry out the moment his fingertips brush my clit. And Klaus knows me so well—he presses down on my slick bud, then pinches it, drawing out the stunning sensations.

My orgasm crashes over me, a wave breaking, but I don't let it pull me under. I want to be present for it all, so I keep my eyes open, looking right at Emmerich. He holds my gaze and watches me fall apart as if I'm the most beautiful, riveting phenomenon he's ever had the pleasure of witnessing.

Then Klaus' movements stutter, and he ruts inside me with quick, shallow thrusts that push him all the way inside me, his hips smacking against my ass. His grip on me tightens, and then he's coming, shaking violently and filling me with hot, thick cum.

I lift my gaze to the sky, a canopy of stars over us, witnessing our love. It's the most perfect moment, with my two mates worshipping me and me loving them fiercely in return.

When Klaus' tremors finally cease, we're both breathing hard. The harness was *definitely* a great idea because my legs wouldn't hold me at all right now. A shudder goes through me, and I moan softly at the feel of Klaus' hard cock still buried in my pussy.

"How is this going to work?" I rasp, then clear my throat to add, "You're too big to fit in the stairway together."

Emmerich chuckles. "I know. We won't attempt it today."

Before I suggest that Klaus could pull out of me and I could walk downstairs on my own two feet, Emmerich undoes the harness on the left side of my body, then moves on to the right. Despite the lack of light, he works deftly, and within a minute, I'm free of the straps that kept me tied to him.

But I don't fall—Klaus supports my weight now, one arm banded around my middle, the other supporting my ass. When he moves, so does his cock inside me, teasing me again.

"I'll prepare the nest," Emmerich announces. He hikes up his pants, still undone from earlier, and disappears down the steps.

A soft yellow glow lights our way as Klaus descends more slowly, taking one step at a time.

"You feel so fucking good around my cock," he murmurs, his nose in my hair. "I wanted to bite you, but we have all night."

I grasp his arm, the one wrapped around my waist, and hold on tight, trying to hold back my whimpers. If he thinks I'm getting close to another orgasm, he'll never let me go.

"Klaus, are you *really* going to stay inside me for the entire weekend?"

"Yes." He stops, drawing in a deep inhale. "Unless you

don't want us to. We will let you use the bathroom, but otherwise, you'll be plugged up tight."

I squirm at his words, my body responding to them instinctively, even as I chide myself for folding so quickly. "All right. But you know human, ah, insemination doesn't work like that, right? I mean, most mammals will mate for a short time, and the sperm travels up all by itself to meet the ovum…"

He starts walking again, and we enter our living room where Emmerich has lit several candles—mostly a concession to my poorer eyesight—and created a true nest of blankets on our bed.

We'd upgraded from the simple mattresses on the floor to a massive custom-made bed that an ice troll friend of theirs built for us. It has enough support for both Klaus' and Emmerich's weight, room for all the pillows and blankets we could ever want, and built-in enchanted metal hoops for nights when Emmerich desires to be put in chains.

Klaus hums in approval at the sight of the cozy bed, then clamps his teeth over the softest spot of my neck, not hard enough to break my skin, just resting his sharp fangs there. He licks me a moment later and says, "We are not taking any chances. You want a baby, and we will do our best to give you one."

Emmerich lies in the center of the nest and motions to Klaus to hand me to him. It's a quick exchange, and within moments, I'm sitting on his hard cock again while Klaus takes the spot beside us.

"I read the book on bats you lent me," Emmerich tells me as I settle on top of him, his warm hands at my waist. "And I learned that some bats create a mating plug when breeding the females."

I goggle at him. "You *what*?"

He nods, his expression serious. "Oh, yes. It's a very good

idea, see. It prevents the seed from leaking out, ensuring better results with mating."

"And you thought—what? That you'd try to do the same?" I smack his hard chest lightly with the back of my hand. "Emmerich! I'm not a bat! And neither are you."

Klaus clears his throat. "No, but the principle applies nevertheless."

"You, too?" I raise my hands in disbelief. "You can't be serious."

Klaus takes my hand and presses a kiss to the inside of my palm. "We would never tease you about this. Having children is something you've always wanted, yes?"

I give him a reluctant nod—not because I'm denying the truth of his statement but because I don't want to fuel his insanity. I *do* want children. Several, if we can. But perhaps not with the use of *mating plugs*. Or using their cocks as a substitute, which I think is their master plan.

"Well, then." Klaus takes the hem of my dress and slowly draws it over my hips, then tugs it higher, exposing my bra, and finally tugs it over my head. "We will do whatever we can to give you what you want. Because we want that future, too. So much."

How can I resist them? Emmerich is looking up at me with such hope, I could never do anything to crush it. If that means having one of their cocks inside me at all times this weekend—and the next, and the next, considering my period schedule—I suppose I'll have to play along.

I move forward, gasping at the feel of Emmerich's thick cock rubbing over all the right places. *What a hardship it will be...*

"I can't believe you read that whole book," I grumble, settling more of my weight on Emmerich so my hips sink all the way down to his. "The part about the mating plugs is right toward the end."

He grips my waist and rocks me up and down his length as if he can't stop himself. "I did. I wanted to know what interests you so. And I have to admit, bats are wonderful."

My throat closes with emotion. He's the kindest, most thoughtful person I've ever met, and I love how he takes care of me. "I'm so glad you think so."

Klaus leans in to kiss me again, even as he fumbles for the clasp of my bra. "But we're better, yes?"

I smile against his lips. "Are you jealous of bats?"

He mock frowns at me. "No, unless you're still hoping one of them will turn into a vampire. Then we might have a problem."

"No, and I only want the two of you, no one else." I tug on his horn and bring his mouth down to mine. "I won't *ever* want anyone else."

He grins, his handsome face lighting up. "Good. Now let's see if we can make that baby."

The End.

Thank you so much for reading *Snowed in with the Gargoyles*! I hope you enjoyed Morgan, Klaus, and Emmerich's story.

Starstruck with the Krampus, another cozy, spicy holiday story is the next book in this series.

. . .

If you haven't read *Stranded with the Kraken* yet, it's available now on Amazon as an ebook and paperback, and in audiobook form on all major audio platforms!

If you'd like to read the first chapter of *Kraken*, turn the page!

To read more of my books, check my "Also by" page - and take your pick of shifters, witches, or monsters!

Happy reading!

xo, Zoe

CHAPTER ONE OF STRANDED WITH THE KRAKEN

ARIELLE

I park my Toyota by the side of the road, near a heap of snow that a plow must have pushed to the side, wondering if I've arrived at the right place. I double-check the maps app, then the last message I got from Jasper, the hot monster guy I'm meeting tonight.

Yep, looks like I'm right where I'm supposed to be. I take a deep breath, then type a message for Jasper in the Bone-R app's chat.

Hey, I'm in front of your house.

Now that I've shut off my car, snowflakes accumulate on the windshield, creating a dusting of white I can't see through. The radio I'd been listening to has been blaring out weather warnings, urging people to get off the roads. It's two days until Christmas, and I debated postponing this rendezvous because of the severe weather warning, but what else am I going to do tonight if not hook up with Jasper? If everything goes to shit and we get snowed in, my home is only about three miles away. I can hike that far if I have to, then pick up my car another day.

It only takes him a moment to reply, so I don't have time to second-guess my decision to be here.

The code for the gate is 122187. Come around the house to the backyard.

Okay, that's a little strange. It's not like Bone-R is an app to share picnic invitations. And it's freaking freezing, with the wind whipping around the car, carrying flurries of snow. I came here with a very specific reason—to hook up with the monster hottie—and he invited me here because he really wants to, er, bone a human.

I sit there for a minute, seriously debating leaving. But I didn't go through the rigorous onboarding process to back out now. I've been chatting with Jasper for days since we first got matched on the app, and I don't want to throw away an opportunity of a real connection, even if it's purely physical.

Still, I text my best friend, Morgan, to let her know where I am. She knows all about Jasper, but I haven't shared his address with her yet. The message remains on unread, which isn't unusual for her at all. Knowing her, she's elbows-deep in her current research project and won't see my text until much later. Still, I like the thought of *someone* knowing where I'm going tonight.

I push open the door, make sure I have pepper spray ready at the top of my purse, and lock my car. I punch in the code at the gate, and the eight-foot-tall sheet of metal slides to the side. This place is a fortress. A shiver of apprehension goes through me, and I feel as if I've strayed far, far away from my small hometown of Clearwater, Maine. I'm entering an entirely new world here, even if I'm actually only at the edge of town.

My slow steps crunch in the thin layer of snow. The gravel pathway leading up to a beautifully restored farmhouse has been shoveled recently, but that won't do much good with the amount of snow coming down. We're no strangers to snowstorms here, but this massive storm system has had weathermen in a frenzy for days.

I stare at the house in awe, because if I had the money to buy and renovate a property, this is what my dream home would look like. Inviting yellow light spills from the tall windows onto the snow, and what I can see of the inside of the house seems tastefully designed and classy. It's nothing like my rental apartment above the general store in town, which looks shabby and worn, no matter how many times I deep clean it using tricks I learned online.

I shake off the melancholy and move toward the side of the house, anticipation rising inside me. At least I didn't arrive to some weird den-type of a monster lair. I'd heard horror stories about women being matched with gargoyles who roost in abandoned stone towers, so arriving at a luxury country home is a good sign. As I near the backyard, strains of music reach me, a low rock ballad that I recognize but can't place exactly. But it's another thing to set me at ease, because Jasper said he wasn't fussy about music, and our shared love of rock concerts was one thing we'd bonded over.

Not that I need bonding to have a one-night stand. I remind myself that this is supposed to be a one-and-done kind of situation. We'll fuck, and then I'll never see him again.

I round the corner of the house, and a wide lawn opens up, with trees lining the edges, creating pockets of darkness. But what catches my attention is a large pool, lit from within, gleaming blue. It's encased in a massive greenhouse-like structure, which wasn't visible from the road. Inside it, strings of fairy lights cast a soft glow over the scene, and Jasper even set up a couple of candles by the water.

I stare at it, unsure of what to do now that I'm here. I glance at the porch, but other than a set of footsteps leading from the patio door down to the covered pool, I don't see anything out of place.

"Arielle, hi," a deep voice says.

I swivel to the right and find the man sitting in a deck chair by the pool, a glass of white wine by his side. The door to the pool is open, signaling he's been waiting for me. He puts away his phone, screen side down, and stands to greet me.

My first sensation at seeing Jasper in the flesh is intense relief. He's even more handsome in person than in the photos he shared with me. Then I flush with the realization that this man is supermodel-hot, his clothes clearly designer, his medium-length hair styled perfectly, and I came here in black jeans and a cute band t-shirt. I picked my combat boots and black puffer jacket because I thought I was meeting a fellow Iron Maiden fan, not a freaking millionaire.

Which Jasper clearly is. Everything about this place screams money, and suddenly I realize just how skewed my vision of tonight has been. I thought I'd have the upper hand, in a way, being human, because monsters have to remain hidden in our society. Now I know nothing could be further from the truth—Jasper is so high above me, class-wise, I have no idea why he thought matching with me on the app was a good idea.

"Hi," I squeak, far too late.

My voice is an octave too high, signaling to him that I'm freaking out. And I haven't even found out what kind of a monster he is. But something pulls me forward, and I take a couple of steps, my boots scuffing on the flagstones leading down to the pool.

"I'm happy you're here," he says, walking toward me

slowly. He's barefoot, which seems strange considering it's wintertime. "Did you have any trouble finding the house?"

I shake my head, still too nervous to speak.

Jasper stops several feet away from me and sniffs the air. His nostrils flare, then he grimaces and retreats a step.

What the hell?

"I'm sorry," he says. "This won't work."

That has me straightening my spine. "Why?"

I look down at myself. Yes, my clothes are much more casual than his, but he saw my photos—this is my go-to everyday uniform, so it's not like I'd misled him. I lift one shoulder slightly to sniff at myself and don't get anything but bodywash and my light perfume. I showered after work, not more than an hour ago, so I have no idea why that would be an issue.

"You're afraid of me," Jasper says, his voice low. "That's not exactly a turn-on."

"I'm not afraid," I reply on instinct. My breath fogs in front of me, a physical manifestation of my lie.

He raises one eyebrow. "No? I can smell it on you."

Oh.

"Well, that's embarrassing," I mutter. Then I straighten my shoulders. "I-I'm not *afraid* of you. Like, I won't scream and start running, if that's what you mean."

Jasper sniffs the air again and doesn't move. "No?"

I shrug. "I'm just…" I motion at the pool, the house, and finally at him. "I'm intimidated."

He cocks his head to the side. "You are? But why?"

I take a tiny step forward before I can stop myself. "You're kidding, right? Everything about this is above my level. I feel like I've walked into a photo shoot for some lifestyle magazine."

"Ah." Jasper palms the back of his neck. His cheeks flush, the change barely visible in the low lighting. "Is it the fairy lights? I thought they'd make the place more cozy, but if it's too much, I can switch them off."

And just like that, some of my apprehension evaporates. He tried to make sure I was cozy?

"No, they're lovely," I say softly. "I don't mind. And that's really thoughtful of you."

He gives me a small smile, and it lights up his face, rendering him instantly more approachable. "So, if you're not about to bolt, would you like a drink?"

Jasper leads me into the pool house. The air inside is warm, like in a tropical greenhouse, and when I stomp snow from my boots, he informs me the floor tiles are heated, which explains his shoeless situation. Feeling a little weird, I unlace my boots and leave them at the entrance along with my socks while Jasper closes the door, shutting us into the cocoon of coziness surrounding the pool. I ask for a glass of wine, and he invites me to sit on the deck chair next to his. I face him, and he turns to me, so our knees are just inches apart, even though we're not sitting together.

"Have you done this before?" he asks. "The Bone-R app, I mean."

"Nope." I shrug off my puffer jacket that's much too warm for this space. "I'm a Bone-R virgin."

I pick up my wineglass and toast him with it, but he doesn't respond. Instead, he stares at me, his lips parted slightly.

"Are you okay?" I ask after a moment.

"Y-you're not a virgin, though, right?" he asks, his voice somewhat strangled.

I laugh. "No, don't worry. That ship has sailed."

He drags a hand over his face and lets out a long exhale. "Thank the gods."

"Why?" I lean forward, leaning my elbows on my knees. "Would that be an issue?"

He grimaces. "What I am is usually an issue even for experienced human women. I wouldn't want to be your first, I don't think, and especially not in a situation like this."

I stare at him, curiosity rising. We've come to the question that's been on my mind for days. "So…what are you?"

Jasper's throat bobs, and he sits back, setting his wineglass down. "You haven't guessed?"

"No?" I think through our conversations. "Should I have?"

A corner of his lips twitches. "I dropped hints for you, hoping we could avoid this conversation."

"Then why didn't you tell me?" I ask, confused.

"You didn't ask," he retorts. "I thought you either knew already or didn't *want* to know."

I set down my glass, too, thinking I need my head straight for this one. "My friend told me it was rude to ask. So I figured you'd tell me eventually." I point at him, then at myself. "I mean, we can hardly do this if you don't tell me, no?"

Jasper purses his lips. "I could fuck you in this form, if that's what you mean."

So he has more than one form? He must be a shifter of some kind. But apart from the gargoyles who can't hide away their wings unless they're wearing glamours, and witches, who only have one human form, he could really be anything. I squint at him. He's not giving me wolf vibes, so I doubt that's it, and he seems to live alone out here, which means he's unlikely to be a bear shifter or any creature who likes pack life. I mentally scroll through the creatures I know exist and settle on the possibility that he's a dragon shifter.

The tall fence around his property and the sense that's he's a loner fit that theory, but why would he hint that he could also fuck me in his other form? Dragons are massive, and if he shifted, he'd freaking rip me apart with his monster dick. I'm pretty sure I ticked HELL NO in the app on any penises larger than twelve inches, thanks.

"Okay." I put my hands up. "You need to tell me what you are. Then we can both make informed decisions."

Jasper sighs. "It'll be easier if I show you."

He stands and walks around the deck chair. His expression falls, though, and I feel a twinge of worry that this is so uncomfortable for him. Without thinking, I snag his hand as he tries to walk past me.

"Hey," I say. "Wait a moment."

He stares down at me, wordless, so I hold on to his hand until he relents and sits next to me. This close to him, I smell his ocean-fresh scent, and it soothes something inside me. I lean in and sniff again, then realize what I'm doing and back away slightly, cheeks heating.

"Sorry," I say. "But, uh, we don't have to do this if you don't want to. I mean, I know we agreed on a hookup, but like you said, if you'd like, you can stay in this form, and we'll see where things lead us." I squeeze his hand, which I still haven't let go. "Unless you want to tell me why this is so hard for you?"

His lips twitch to the side, and he gives me a wry smile. "All right. Imagine you meet a pretty girl." He reaches out and wraps a strand of my dark hair around his fingers, then tugs lightly. "But the moment she sees your true shape, she turns tail and disappears as fast as she can."

I wince. "Someone did that? Is that why you reacted so strongly when you scented me?"

He dips his chin in a nod. "Yeah. Imagine that happened *every* time you met someone you liked. I don't want to traumatize another beautiful woman."

"Right." I take another deep inhale of his clean, intoxicating scent. "So…do you want to keep it a secret?" I glance down at our interlaced fingers. "Do you want to fuck me as a human?"

He closes his eyes and lets out a shuddering breath. "If it means you won't run away…"

Fuck, this guy has some issues. I don't know what the deal was with the other women he's met, or how hideous his true form is. I could accept his offer for a human-shaped quickie. He's gorgeous, and I'm fairly sure he called me beautiful just now. So we'd likely get each other off, then go our separate ways. But I don't think I can do that to him either. It would be another rejection—even if it doesn't look that way on the surface. And if I leave now, I'll spend the rest of my life wondering about what could have been.

And maybe we both need this. Maybe we need each other, even if it's only for a night. After all, everyone else is preparing for a white Christmas with their families, and we're on a Bone-R date. I don't know if Jasper had any other goals besides having a fuck buddy, but I agreed to meet tonight in part because I wanted to forget about the fact that I don't have anyone to spend the holidays with.

Oof. I haven't admitted that to myself until now, not in so many words.

"Listen," I say. "I can't promise you for sure I'll want to have sex with you after you show me your true form. I've never done this, and even though I filled out that questionnaire, I don't *really* know what my hard limits are. Okay?"

He frowns but says, "I understand."

"But," I continue before he can say anything more, "I *can* promise that I won't run away. Or scream."

I bite my lip to stop myself from babbling out something more, because it's on him to decide now.

Jasper remains silent for a long minute, his gaze roaming from my eyes to my lips, down to where my band t-shirt has slipped off my shoulder, and back to my face. His fingers tighten on mine, and he dips his head, giving me plenty of time to move away. Then he closes his lips over mine, the kiss tentative and soft at first. I lift my chin and angle my head to the side, giving us room to explore, and when I part my lips for him, he deepens the kiss, taking over.

He brings his hand up to cup the back of my neck, his thumb caressing my jaw, and it's the best kiss I've ever had, slow and thorough, as if he's mapping me, learning how to seduce all my senses. The taste of him is exquisite, the sweet bite of the white wine mixing with something more potent. If I didn't know better, I'd say he tastes a little salty, but the effect is amazing, sort of like the creamiest peanut butter.

I want to stay right here and suck on his tongue until the end of time, but Jasper tears himself off me, breathing hard.

"Fuck," he says. "This might be more complicated than I thought."

Read *Stranded with the Kraken* now!

ALSO BY ZOE ASHWOOD

CLEARWATER MONSTERS
(paranormal Christmas monster romance)

Stranded with the Kraken

Snowed in with the Gargoyles

Starstruck with the Krampus

BELLHAVEN CLAN
(orc fantasy romance)

Her Orc Mate - freebie!

Her Orc King

Her Orc Guardian

Her Orc Warrior

Her Orc Protector

Her Orc Husband

Her Orc Gentleman

His Orc Lady

Box Set #1

Box Set #2

SEA DRAGONS OF AMBER BAY
(Reverse Harem Romance, complete)

Tempted

Ensnared

Seduced

Box Set

NORA MOSS

(Reverse Harem Romance, complete)

Jinxed in Love, freebie

Cursed in Love

Captured in Love

Freed in Love

Box Set

NORSE SEA DRAGONS duet

(Paranormal Romance, complete)

Deep Sea Kiss

Deep Sea Love

ICE PLANET RENDU

(Sfi-Fi Alien Romance, complete)

Cold Attraction

Cold Temptation

Cold Seduction

SHIFT SERIES

(Paranormal Romance)

Bearly Married, freebie

Trust the Wolf

Truth or Bear

Make Him Howl

ABOUT THE AUTHOR

Zoe Ashwood writes cinnamon roll heroes, no matter how loud they growl.

While she's always been a reader, Zoe's writing used to be limited to diary scribbles and bad (really *bad*) teenage poetry. Then she participated in NaNoWriMo 2015 and never looked back.

A million words later, she's still in love with the art of making up stories—and making her characters fall in love.

Zoe is happily married to her best friend and has two boys who are as stubborn as they're cute. They also have a dog who has more fur than sense but is luckily too damn adorable to be turned into a rug.

The best way of keeping in touch is her newsletter (at zoeashwood.com/newsletter) of Facebook Group (Zoe's Cabin). You can also find her on social media:

- patreon.com/zoeashwood
- bookbub.com/authors/zoe-ashwood
- amazon.com/Zoe-Ashwood/e/B07K3T8QXH
- tiktok.com/@zoeashwood

Printed in Dunstable, United Kingdom

65066667R00139